Wagons to the Wilderness

A Story of Westward Expansion

By SAMUEL HOPKINS ADAMS

Illustrated by Norman Guthrie Rudolph

Cecile Matschat, *Editor*
Carl Carmer, *Consulting Editor*

THE JOHN C. WINSTON COMPANY

Philadelphia · Toronto

Wagons to the Wilderness

To my young friend and—I hope—
constant reader, William Waight Elliott,
this book is inscribed.

"Flying Stores"

THE story of the westward-rolling wagons in the early days of our nation's development is a record of courage and initiative that we like to think of as characteristic of all of us as a people. It holds many memories—of the great wheels turning in axle-deep dust, of river waters dashing the wagon boxes downstream, of canyons so choked with rocks that progress was inch by inch, of fire-lit bivouacs suddenly endangered by the circling attacks of whooping Indians.

After the explorers came the trappers, and with the second wave of trappers—the wagons. They were the conveyers of "flying stores" to carry on profitable trade with the Indians, the suppliers of permanent settlements that would send Western harvests to the Eastern markets, the forerunners of railroads and trucks and planes which would one day follow the selfsame trails they had traveled. In this story of one wagon train you may read the story of them all, a tale of the dogged persistence of brave men who literally fought their way west—against the opposition of nature, of wild men defending their homes, of money-mad villains of their own race—land pirates who would steal and kill for profit. The whole nation owes much to the fearless wagoners of its past.

C. C.

CONTENTS

CHAPTER   PAGE

"Flying Stores" vii

1. The Atajo 1

2. The Recruit 11

3. House Cleaning 24

4. Trail Politics 42

5. The Cibola Man 57

6. The Test 64

7. Bad Luck Day 74

8. The Jumping-Off Place 82

9. Halfway 93

10. The Troublemaker 101

11. Mirage 110

12. Trap Lore 121

13. Death at the Ford 136

14. The Patron 152

15. Santa Fe 165

CHAPTER 1

The Atajo

FRANKLIN, Missouri, in 1822, was the outfitting place for the great wilderness of the West. Further along the sunset trail were lonely houses built like forts, a day's travel apart, and a few huddles of buildings that called themselves towns. Franklin was the end of settled civilization. It was the last landing for the upriver boats from St. Louis bringing merchandise. It was also the farthest-west wagon stop in the United States.

Franklin had a post office, a jail, three stores, ten saloons, nothing resembling a hotel, and no school. It claimed a population of six hundred, of which eight were women and one a boy. The boy on this hot August afternoon was fishing in

1

the Big Muddy, as the Missouri River was locally called. He was intent upon the business in hand. It meant supper for him.

The heavy rumble of a wagon pulling up at the wharf annoyed him. It might scare the fish now nibbling cautiously at his bait. The wagon stopped.

The bobbin dipped under. The fisherman struck. There was a brief struggle before a shiny blue-black catfish was flopping on the boards. A voice from the high wagon-seat said:

"Fresh fish! I ain't tasted fresh fish since I left Saint Loo."

The boy turned to look at the speaker. He saw a tall, spare, loose-jointed figure that appeared to be all corded muscle, a face as swarthy as an Indian's where the heavy, brown beard did not mask it, and a pair of quiet, gray eyes below which jutted a powerfully beaked nose. The stranger's dress was rough and warm, but of the best frontier quality. Across one shoulder a gaping triangular rent in the leather showed red flannel beneath. His voice had the low, slow level of those who do not have much opportunity to talk, as he said:

"I'd certes admire to eat fried fish again. How much you reckon that fella would weigh?"

The boy lifted his catch by the gills. "Three pounds," he said.

"Take sixpence for it?"

Two cents a pound was liberal for river fish. "Yes, sir," the fisherman said.

The other said, "Belong here?"

"I've been living here awhile," the boy replied.

"Know Captain Mabbitt?"

"Salt Lick Mabbitt? Everybody knows him."

"Charles L. Mabbitt. Don't know about the Salt Lick."

"They call him that because he's a salter," the boy explained. "Tracks out salt wells from the animal trails and prospects 'em."

"Might be the same man. Might not." The stranger drew from his pocket one of the printed sheets known as broadsides and blinked at it. "You wouldn't know anybody that could read this for me, would you?"

"Yes, sir," the boy answered. "I can."

The man regarded him with surprise and some admiration. "Dotch me!" he said. "Got schoolin', have you? Take a look." He handed over the paper. "My eyes are sore," he explained. "Not that I'm any too handy at reading anyways," he added frankly.

The broadside carried an advertisement:

Wanted: I am raising a Company of Men destined to the Westward for the purpose of trading for Horses and Mules and capturing Wild Animals of every Kind. Only men with full Outfits need apply. Fee $10.00. Up to August 15 I can be found at Gilligan's Grove, down river from Franklin.

CHARLES L. MABBITT.

The man looked disappointed. "Wild animals, huh?"

"Yes, sir; that's what it says."

"Nothing about Santa Fe?"

"Not in this paper."

"How far is this Gilligan's Grove?"

"Half a mile."

"What's your name?"

"Esty Lang."

"Howdy, Esty Lang. Ever hear of Beaver Jim Jones?"

"No, sir; I don't believe I have."

"Well, tell the truth and shame the Devil. I'm him," Mr. Jones said. He tossed his fish into the wagon, reached the high seat in one jump as lithe and easy as a cat, and drove down the dusty street, the torn sleeve flapping in the breeze.

"See you again, mebbe," he threw over his shoulder at the boy.

Esty went back to his fishing.

Next morning Esty Lang walked out to Gilligan's Grove. A heavy cloud of dust overhung the clearing where the Mabbitt camp was pitched. Beneath it, horses, mules, and men in a hurry milled about. There were wagons, covered and uncovered, carts and sledges, and a few one-man tents. Merchandise of many kinds was strewn on the ground. It seemed to Esty that half of the

population of Franklin must be there looking on.

He had learned in the hard school of kicks and cuffs that where men were busy, small boys would better keep out of the way. Near the hitching rail on one side of the open space grew a hard maple. Esty shinnied up it and found himself a reserved seat on a comfortable branch overlooking the busy scene. This, he thought, must be like a circus. He had never seen a circus, but he had read the splendid advertisements in the newspapers which came in from the East now and then. He would like to have had a part in all the bustle and activity, but saw no chance. Nobody spoke to him. Nobody noticed him. They were all too busy. The boy felt lonesome.

A man came around the end of a Pittsburgh wagon and seated himself on the tongue. It was the buyer of Esty's fish. From a small leather bag he took a needle which he threaded. He shucked off his leather-and-cloth jacket and set to work to mend the tear on the shoulder. In his powerful fingers the needle seemed out of place. He sewed diligently but clumsily, breathing hard.

A chunky man on a palomino pony pulled up with an exclamation. He wore a brilliantly beaded coat with a polished silver star on it.

"I'm a sidehill wampus if it ain't Beaver Jim Jones!"

The sewer looked up. "Do I know you?" His face lighted. "Jumpin' Jehoshaphat! It's Tom Avery. Howdy, Tom! Where'd you get the tin twinkler?"

The other affectionately polished the star which marked him as the town marshal. "I'm the Law," he said. "Thought you was up the Oregon Trail."

"I was. I'm back."

"Still an *engagé* for John Jacob Astor? Or was it the Hudson's Bay Company?"

"Neither, now. I'm a freeman this last year."

The listening boy knew enough frontier talk to understand. Mr. Jones had been an engagé, a hired trapper, working for one of the great fur companies as a member of a large band. He had quit and become a freeman, an independent.

The marshal said, "What fetches you here? Joining up with Salt Lick Mabbitt's atajo?"

"That's me. Santa Fe or bust."

"Know what you'd better do when you get through with that job?" He pointed to the half-mended tear.

"No. What?"

"Take a fresh needleful and sew your scalp

on tight," the marshal said with an unpleasant gesture.

"I've met up with Injuns before," the trapper returned unconcernedly. "I'd rather parlay with a tribe of 'em than tackle a job like this," he added, scowling down at it, as the marshal waved his hand and rode on.

Esty Lang took a long breath and said, "Mister, can I say something?"

Mr. Jones looked up. "Why, it's the catfisher! Say your say."

"That over-and-under stitch won't hold."

"Huh! Think you could do it better?"

"Yes, sir. What's it worth?"

The tall man looked at him hard, then laughed. "Trader, huh? Well, you're in the right place. This is a trading outfit. A fip be about right?"

"Yes, sir," Esty said quickly. Fivepence was more than he would have dared to ask.

"I can't work that silver-nosed blunt on leather, though," he went on. "It's the wrong kind of needle."

"Dig into my possible-sack." Mr. Jones pointed to a large bag of heavy cloth swinging from a hook above the wagon seat. A frontiersman's possible-sack was supposed to hold every

small object that he might possibly need on the
long trail, from a plug of kinnikinnick tobacco to
a mold for casting tallow-dip candles. "You've
set yourself a stent. I'll leave you to it." He
walked away with the long, noiseless stride of
the mountain man.

When the owner came back, the coat was
spread out to air on the wagon tongue. He in-
spected it, nodded, and handed the boy a coin.

"Right handy for yourself, ain't you!" he commented.

"I've had to be," Esty said gravely. "Or I wouldn't eat."

"Got no folks?"

"No, sir."

"How've you been living?"

"Odd jobs."

"Like it?"

"No, sir."

The trapper considered. Presently he asked, "Ever been out on trail?"

"Not west of here."

"Think you'd like it?"

Esty's heart was in his throat. "With you?" he managed to ask.

"With the outfit. With the atajo." He made a sweeping gesture which took in the whole encampment. "Don't reckon on me to look after you. You'd be on your own."

"Yes, sir," Esty said.

"Want to try it?"

"I'd admire to!"

"Come back tomorrow morning early. We'll go see the boss."

CHAPTER 2

The Recruit

SUNUP found Esty at Gilligan's Grove. The camp was already busy. Small fires of chips and twigs burned and snapped while over them the men prepared breakfast. Beaver Jim Jones had already finished his. He was carefully washing and drying the tin plate, tin cup, two-tined steel fork, and long-bladed skinning knife which made up his entire tableware. This done, he hung out his coarse towel of fustian to dry, restored his knife to his belt, and stowed away the other utensils. He was a neat and orderly man, was Mr. Jones.

He nodded a greeting to the boy and led the way across the enclosure, where the nation's flag,

11

with its twenty-four stars crinkling in the breeze above a large tent, marked the expedition's headquarters. The tent flap was already drawn back. Captain Mabbitt's workday began early. From within issued sounds of a dispute. An angry voice was protesting. A slow, firm, quiet one put an end to argument.

"I said No. And when I say No, it's No."

A heavy-built fellow, his face red with rage, stamped out, almost bumping into Mr. Jones. He stopped and shook his fist at the tent.

"I gotta mind to get my ten dollars back and quit."

"What's wrong, Hoyler?" the trapper asked.

"He's interferin' with my trade," Hoyler growled.

"Barrel trade?" the other asked.

"What if it is? Do you know any brisker line of business than whisky?"

"Not for Injuns," the trapper replied. "An Injun will sell his horse or his squaw for your rotgut, that's true. But that don't make it a right trade."

"You another of these mealy-mouthed psalm singers?" the trader demanded contemptuously.

The other refused to be roiled. "You can lose your scalp to a whisky-crazy redskin if you want to. I aim to keep mine. Captain Mabbitt is right."

Hoyler strode away. Mr. Jones thrust his head into the tent opening. "Busy, boss?" he inquired.

"I'm always busy," the leader answered. "Come in."

He was seated at a rough deal table, poring over a hand-inked map. He lifted his head.

"Ever hear of two rivers crossing each other at right angles, Jim?" he asked.

"Not in any parts I ever traveled, Captain," the visitor said.

"Well, that's what they do on this map," the captain said, hammering it with his fist. "Drat these trail-finders! I'd almost rather travel by the sun and stars . . . Hullo, what you got there?" he asked, peering at Esty.

"He wants to join up," the trapper said.

"Huh!" the leader grunted. "Stand out there, boy."

Esty stepped up to the table. A pair of grotesquely uneven eyes in a rugged face beneath a mop of red hair stared at him. They were so cross-eyed that they made Esty feel lopsided.

"Too young," Captain Mabbitt pronounced.

"I'm almost fourteen, sir," Esty said politely.

"He's smart, boss," the trapper put in. "He can read and write."

The big boss grinned. "So can I. But not without sweatin'. And we ain't takin' no liberaries along this trip."

"He can figure, too," the other persisted.

The boss looked from the bearded face to the smooth one. "What's he to you, Jones?"

"Nothing by kin."

"Then what do you want him along for?"

"Look you, Cap," the trapper said. "I had one once. He'd have been about this spratling's age."

Captain Mabbitt's hard face softened. All the frontier knew of the tragedy years before on the Oregon Trail. Jones's young wife and son had been run down and eaten by a pack of wolves on a winter fur-range.

"I'd like to oblige you, Jim," the captain said, "but this is a tough trail. He couldn't carry his weight, even if there was any place for him."

"I thought he might help the *madre*, boss."

"No," the captain said and turned back to his map.

Esty felt like crying in his disappointment. He said in a half-whisper to his friend:

"If a lady can stand it, why can't I?"

The trapper stared. "Lady? What lady?"

"Somebody's mother. Didn't you say something about my helping the madre? Madre is Spanish for mother."

A great burst of laughter checked him. "Madre is camp lingo for the cook," the trapper explained, when his mirth had subsided, "and our Cookee is nobody's mother."

Captain Mabbitt cut in. He had overheard. He called to the boy.

"Come back here. You speak Mexicano?"

"Poquito," Esty said. "A little."

"Where'd you learn it?"

"My mother was part Spanish."

"Go out and find Gregory. Tell him I want the *cargador* who came in from the Picketwire country."

Esty found Anson Gregory, a lanky Kentuckian, who was the leader's assistant and right-hand man.

"The cargador?" Gregory said. "That's him over there playing the guitar."

The handsome young Mexican readily accompanied the messenger to the tent. He bowed to Captain Mabbitt with grave formality and waited. The captain pointed to Esty.

"You parla some Español to this brat," he directed.

The smiling Mexican addressed several questions to the lad. Esty replied without too much difficulty, while the leader listened, frowning.

"Well!" he said impatiently. "How is he? Pretty good at the lingo?"

"Esta bueno," the cargador said. "He ees alri'."

"Thank you," the captain said, dismissing him. He addressed Esty with military sharpness. "Stand there. Answer up. What's your name?"

"Esty Lang."

"When I ask your name, I want your name, not your initials. What's the *S* stand for and never mind the *T*."

"That's my name. E-s-t-y," the boy answered quietly.

"Humph! How old did you say you was?"

"Thirteen, sir."

"Don't look it. Can you ride?"

"Yes, sir."

"Pack?"

"I want to learn."

"Where are your folks?"

"I haven't got any."

"Sure you want to join up?"

"Yes, sir."

The captain called to the trapper, who had

stepped outside. "Jones, will you be bespoken for the lad?"

"No, sir," came the answer. "I've told him he'd be on his own."

"All right," the captain barked. He drew out a sheet of paper covered with writing, laboriously amended it and pushed it toward the waiting boy.

"Sign there," he said. "Read it out so as Beaver Jim can hear."

The document provided that the said Esty Lang should be assistant to the cook and also do "sundry chores, various and unspecified." He was also to act as interpreter should they encounter Mexicans. For these duties he was to be paid five dollars a month and found. The "found" meant that he would receive his share of the camp rations: tea, sugar, salt, flour, and bacon as long as it lasted. When it gave out, there would be such meat as the hunters brought in.

Mr. Jones listened carefully. "Five a month," he commented, to the boy. "Good pay. Come along. We'll find the madre."

Gid (short for Gideon) Prouty, the cook, did not indeed look like anybody's mother. He proved to be a fat, red-faced, mustached man of

thirty with a set of the shiniest teeth that Esty had ever seen. Gid was very proud of his teeth and delighted in telling how he had won them from a St. Louis scow pilot in a poker game. They were, he declared, genuine mineral succedaneum, "wuth twenty-five dollars if they're wuth a cent," and would sometimes add that they were better than the original set which a mule had kicked in.

Cookee welcomed his new helper cordially and assured him that the work would be easy.

"Practically nuthin' to do," he said. "Git up at five. Collect chips for the fire. Unpack the vittles. Git water for the bilin' kittles. Gimme a hand with the cookin'. Clean up the kittles and spits. I'll learn you how to use spike grass for that. Pack 'em up. Mebbe help me lead the bell mare that always goes ahead of the mules. Might be a little wagon-tinkerin' in the rough places if you're handy with tools. The horsemen would expect you to keep their saddles mended. Then after we set camp you'll have plenty of time to take the stock out to feed and fetch 'em in later. Of course, you'll take your turn on guard duty. I ain't sayin' nothin' of the odd jobs. You can tend to *them* any time. Yes, it's a nice easy life for a growin' boy."

Esty reflected that, while five dollars a month was certainly a generous wage, he would probably earn every cent of it.

Outside in the sunshine the men were taking it easy. The morning tasks were finished. A group of those who had signed up for the Mabbitt expedition were gathered about the wagons. They were already marked men: "Mabbitt's men," committed to a perilous adventure. Bets were laid at even money that they would never come back.

If they were headed for danger, they certainly did not seem to be worrying about it, Esty thought, as he watched them at their relaxations. Four were squatted on a brightly woven blanket playing cards. One of them hummed a song of the trail:

> *"I'll give my hoss*
> *A feed of hay,*
> *And hit the dust*
> *For Santa Fe."*

Everywhere Esty heard the name Santa Fe repeated. Nobody in the atajo had ever been there. Yet all seemed to take it for granted that they were bound for the mysterious city nearly a thousand miles away.

Anson Gregory walked across the flat and addressed the group. "Any of you want to learn how to pack a mule?"

Several looked up, interested.

"The boss has got a couple of experts to show us how. Over in front of his tent."

The big fellow who had quarreled with Captain Mabbitt growled:

"Oh, go teach your grandmother to suck eggs."

"Know it all, do you, Hoyler?" Gregory said good-humoredly. "All right. Nobody has to come that don't want to."

He walked away. Nothing happened. The card players finished their deal. Nobody was going to hurry *them*. The others watched for a while, stretched, yawned, and ambled away as if they were accepting Gregory's suggestion only because they had nothing better to do.

Esty, observing, thought maybe it was the proper way to behave. Then he shrewdly reflected that what was all right for a grown man might not be so good in a boy. He trotted after Anson Gregory.

The ground before the captain's tent was strewn with merchandise of all sorts. Half a dozen mules stood with drooping ears and uninterested eyes. Among them moved the cargador who had tested Esty's Spanish and another young Mexican, in the beribboned and bemetaled dress of their nation.

"There's no slicker *arrieros* (packers) on the plains than these two," Gregory informed the crowd. "They can pack a mula de carga so easy

and gentle he thinks he's in stable, being curried
down. Watch close now, boys." He addressed
the taller of the youths. "Go to it, cargador."

Esty watched with all his eyes while the Mexicans selected a mule. Standing, one on either
side, they put in place the sheepskin pad stuffed
with hay, set the heavy saddle over it, and bound
all firmly with woven grass bandages. Now the
twin cargo bags were set in place. Working with
even movements the arrieros filled the bags with
merchandise for the trail. The weight was kept
balanced. With a long rope they wove in and
out, an exact and scientific pattern which held
everything tight. Having examined the knots,
the cargador gave the animal a friendly thwack
on its smooth rump.

"Vaya, mula!" he cried, and the mule, with a
little fillip of his hind legs, trotted away.

"Exactly three hundred pounds," Gregory,
the lecturer, said. "That's all a mule will carry
without making a fuss. Don't ask me how the
arrieros reckon the exact weight without scales.
Don't ask them, either, for they won't tell you . . .
Trot out another, cargador."

The second animal was nervous. It kept rolling its head and fidgeting with its feet, which
made the work of loading difficult. For a time

the Mexican tried soothing words; the mule continued to prance. The cargador called to a companion on the side lines.

"Tapajos, Miguel."

A leather strap with two flaps was handed to him. He slipped it over the restlessly weaving head. The flaps settled over the eyes. The mule instantly relaxed and stood quiet.

"See that, hombres," the voice of the lecturer said. "Never beat a mule. If he gets skittish, blindfold him and what have you got? A woolly lamb."

As the exhibition continued, Esty tried to follow the ins and outs of the rope. The movements of the expert hands were too quick for him. Mr. Jones's quiet voice, back of him, asked:

"Think you could do it, youngling?"

"No, sir."

"Not sure I could, myself. That last was the diamond hitch. Best pack-hitch in the world, and hardest to learn. I'll show you an easier one." He looked about him. "The show's over," he said. "Ready to go?"

"Yes, sir."

"All right. Hay-foot, straw-foot, hep! We'll p'int for town and lay in some trade."

CHAPTER 3

House Cleaning

BARNEY's Last Chance Emporium was a one-story shack of rough cottonwood logs. Esty and Mr. Jones made their way to it through the dust of the roadway. There were no sidewalks in Franklin.

In the hot sunshine outside, a crowd milled and jostled and gossiped. There were plainsmen, traders, trappers, ox-teamers with long quirts, muleteers, wagoners, buffalo hunters, gamblers, rivermen, prospectors, half-breeds jingling with bright metal beads and ornaments, loafers, mountain men, heavy-bearded and silent, gold seekers, arrieros, a tinker with his hand forge, a knife grinder with his whetstone on wheels, and Mrs. Postmaster Huff, very finefied in a quilted kiss-me-quick bonnet with blue satin streamers which she had just bought as the latest wrinkle from the fashionable East. She addressed Mr. Jones.

"You with Salt Lick Mabbitt's outfit?"

"Yes, ma'am."

"Got a package for him at the office. Marked 'Valuable. Handle with Care.' Eighty-four cents postage to pay."

"I'll stop for it, ma'am."

Her husband came up. "Hear you Mabbitt fellows are buying out the store."

"I don't reckon that Mr. Barney is going to get poor on our business," the trapper replied pleasantly.

"What beats me," Mrs. Postmaster Huff said, "is how you figure to transport all that tonnage."

"Part muleback; mostly wagons," Mr. Jones replied.

"Wagons!" The word passed through the crowd in every accent of surprise and disbelief. "Did he say *wagons?*"

"Did' ja hear that, Tom?" someone called to the town marshal who had reined in his palomino at the edge of the crowd. "Salt Lick Mabbitt's forming up a *wagon* train for the outtrail. What do you think of that?"

"I think he's loco," the marshal declared. "Plumb exalted in the head."

"Then I'm crazy, too," Mr. Jones said with a smile. "I'm driving my wagon in the atajo."

"Wanna bet?" a one-armed man said. "You'll not get as far as Council Grove. Why, hombre, there's never a wheel turned west of the Big Muddy."

"There's always got to be a first time," Mr. Jones said placidly.

The marshal spoke up. "Look you, Jim. You only know that country as far as the Oregon Trail fork. Wait till you strike the rough going, up past the Arkansas River. It's tough even for mules. Wagons? Why, you ain't got the chance of a jack rabbit in a rattlesnake's hole. I tell you, it's never been done. Not on wheels."

The one-armed man came in with his bit. "What'll the Injuns do to a slow-moving wagon train? Pawnees and Shawnees, Arapahoes, Paiutes and Comanches—there's more redskins between here and the Rockies than there are ticks on a buffalo calf's hump."

"The more Injuns, the more trade," Mr. Jones said.

The postmaster's wife pointed a finger at Esty. "And you're taking that lad out there to be scalped by Indians and bitten by rattlesnakes and chewed up by grizzlies! It's a sin, that's what it is."

"He wants to be a trader, don't you, boy?" the trapper said.

"Arrows for bullets, that's all the trade he'll get," a weazened prospector said.

"Oh, I dunno," an ox driver put in. "There's plenty beaver in them rivers, I guess."

"And plenty gold in the ranges." Storekeeper Barney had come out. "Salt Lick Mabbitt waste his time on furs? Don't you believe it. Gold's his mark." ,

The word, as always, started excited discussion.

"Gold's a jobbernow's game," a riverman said. "No gold out there."

"Jobbernow, yourself!" a mule wrangler promptly contradicted him. "Certes, there's gold. Didn't Captain Zebulon Pike find it out behind that high peak of his?"

"Not him," the marshal said. "That was Jim Pursley. Over north of the Picketwire." So the trailsmen called the Purgatoire River. "And nobody ever could find the place again."

"Who wants gold!" a bedraggled loafer grunted. "Jewels and gems. That's the ticket!

Pick 'em up anywhere; bigger'n your big toe-nail."

"All you got to do is to fill your pockets and take 'em to Santa Fe," a sarcastic voice said.

"Goin' to take the short cut across the Jornada?" the one-armed man asked.

"Jornada del Muerto," the shopkeeper added. "The Journey of Death. That's as good a place to leave your bones as any other, I guess. Mr. Jones, your trade is stacked up inside."

The trapper and the boy followed him to a corner where the floor was covered with bales of cloth, tools, kegs, and sacks of various sizes.

"How much does she weigh?" the customer asked.

"Twenty-three-fifty pounds," Mr. Barney answered.

"That's about all I want to pack." He turned to Esty. "You goin' to deal?"

"I've got about fourteen dollars put by," the boy said.

"Injun trade for you," Mr. Jones advised. "Small, light and fancy. There wouldn't be room for anything big. I'll rent you a shelf to hold it. Three foot by one. Five dollars." Esty's face fell. "Payable after you market your stuff," he added and Esty's expression lightened.

Mr. Jones advised on his companion's pur-
chases; mostly trinkets, bright-hued beads and
ornaments. On one of the shop shelves stood a
supply of musical odds and ends: cheap fiddles
and guitars, a few small drums, a flute or two
and some smaller instruments. Esty pointed to
a box of jew's-harps.

"How much?" he asked.

"Fifty cents apiece."

"How many have you got?"

The salesman counted out nine.

"Give you three dollars for the lot."

"They're slow moving," the man admitted. "Make it three-fifty and it's a trade."

Mr. Jones had been looking on in surprise. Now he said, "Business is business, and I don't aim to interfere with yours. But what you're going to do with nine of those articles beats me. I never heard that Injuns like music."

"They don't."

"Then what good's a jew's-harp to 'em?"

"It tickles their teeth. They like it."

"Well, dotch *me*!" the trapper exclaimed. "How did you find that out?"

Esty explained that a Kiowa chief who knew a little English had come to town and heard him playing on his instrument. Esty had lent it to him. At the first twang a look of astonished delight had spread over the Kiowa's face. The owner's best endeavors could not get the jew's-harp back from him. It ended with the Indian's paying a dollar for the delightful novelty.

What remained of Esty's cash he invested in fishhooks and lines. To Mr. Jones's comment that there would be no Indian market for those—the Indians speared or trapped their fish—Esty replied merely that he'd heard there were a lot of rivers along the trail.

The day's trade ended with Mr. Jones buying

a bucket of potash which he took with him,
leaving the other goods to be called for.

Besides being the postmaster's wife, Mrs.
Thad Huff was the nearest thing to a newspaper
in Franklin. In other words, she was the town
gossip. Anxious not to miss anything of interest,
she took pains to be at the post-office counter
when Beaver Jim Jones and Esty called for Captain Mabbitt's parcel. As she made the change
for Mr. Jones's dollar, she said archly:

"You don't gull me with that fahdoodle about
beaver pelts and hoss trading."

"No, ma'am," Mr. Jones said. "I don't aim to
fool nobody."

Mrs. Huff flattened a plump finger against the
side of her nose. "Cibola," she half-whispered.

Mr. Jones looked innocent and puzzled.

"The Seven Lost Cities," she went on. "Don't
let on to me that you don't know what I'm talking about."

"Lost Cities?" Mr. Jones said. "Why, yes, I've
heard stories about 'em. Might be true. Might
be lies. I'd say the latter."

"More men's gone to look for them than ever
came back," she said ominously.

"Not me," Mr. Jones said. "I haven't lost any
cities. I'm a beaver man."

Perceiving that there was little to be had from the trapper on the subject of Cibola, the lady tried another topic.

"Hear you was buying potash at Barney's store."

"Yes."

"Trade?"

"House cleaning."

Her eyebrows went up. "It wouldn't be you that bought the Ferrier boys' outfit, would it?"

"Yes," Mr. Jones said shortly.

She pursed her lips and emitted a prolonged "whee-ee-ee-ew!" Esty thought it a very unlady-like performance. Apparently she would have followed up her whistle with further comment. Mr. Jones gave her no chance. With a curt "Good day to you, ma'am," he took up the package and left the place.

At the official tent, Captain Mabbitt welcomed the parcel with evident relief. He stripped off the wrappings to reveal a metal box labeled "Genuine Kine-Pox." Mr. Jones spelled out the words.

"Vaccination stuff, huh?" he said with interest.

"Yes," the leader answered. "I wouldn't move a rod without it."

They returned to the Pittsburgh, where its owner brought out a bucket and churned up his potash with water. From a corner he took a large soft rag, and set himself to his cleaning work. Esty offered to help and was rather surprised at the curtness with which his friend told him to keep out of the wagon. He strolled across the clearing to find Gid Prouty, who might be able to explain this strange business. The madre walked back with him, talking as they went.

"Beaver Jim got that Pittsburgh mortal cheap. Sixty skins, they say." A "skin," in trail language, meant a beaver pelt reckoned at five dollars. "That Pittsburgh," the speaker pointed at the wagon, "is wuth five hundred and the four hosses four hundred more. Jim gets the whole outfit for three hundred. Slick trade, huh? Know why?"

"No," Esty said.

"The Ferrier boys that owned it died inside it of the spots. Black spots."

They had reached the place. Mr. Jones's face appeared at the front of the wagon. "What have you been telling the boy?" he demanded.

"Nothin' much," the cook answered uneasily. "Just thought he'd oughta know about the smallpox."

The trapper noted Esty's pale face. "Are you scared, lad?" he asked.

"No, sir. That isn't it," the boy said in a shaking voice.

"What is it, then?"

"Dad and my ma both died of the spots."

"That's bad," the other said gravely and kindly. "Don't get into the wagon," he added, "till I get it all washed out."

"I hear Captain Mabbitt's got some of this newfangled stuff they call kine-pox," said the madre. News got around the encampment swiftly. "They say it will fix the wust case of the spots. They rub it into your arm and it swells you up like a balloon but it don't kill you. Leastways, not often, I guess," he added.

Smallpox at that time was the scourge of the trails. Whole bands of explorers were wiped out by it. Some of those who knew of vaccination believed it to be a magical sort of cure. Others accepted horrifying stories that it caused people to grow horns and run about on all fours, bellowing. Captain Mabbitt, who had been through an epidemic in the East, was a firm believer in vaccination. It became known in the encampment that he regarded the box of kine-pox as his most valued possession.

Mr. Jones's final operation was to sluice down the floor of the Pittsburgh. This done, he hitched up the horses, Esty helping him. The trapper climbed to the high seat. Esty clambered up beside him.

They pulled up at the store, and the loading began. Esty marveled at the skill with which the owner packed. Not an inch of space was wasted. The trade goods were stowed first; bright-colored calicos, merinos, and sarsenets; cheap tools,

knives, saws, files, rope, pails, brooms, tobacco, starch, and candlewicking, with a sprinkling of beads and ribbons. The food shelf carried a careful selection of necessaries; salt, sugar, flour, pepper (at a shocking price), a little dried corn, coffee, tea, and unhulled rice. A flitch of bacon was hung from the top of the wagon. No fresh meat was taken; they would shoot their own. Vegetables they hoped to get in trade from friendly tribes.

In a corner stood the trapper's musket, and above it was stowed powder, lead, and a mold for casting bullets. Esty's rented shelf was filled to overflowing with his queerly assorted trade. It caused Mr. Jones a great deal of amusement but he made no further comment. One last purchase was made by Esty. Getting up before sunrise, he had found three jobs sweeping out taprooms at two bits apiece. With this seventy-five cents he filled the possible-bag of coarse humhum which the generous storekeeper had given him. Every useful knickknack he could think of went into it; needles and thread; bits of cloth and leather for patching; five different kinds of string; a box of hand-forged nails; two candles; a lump of chalk for figuring, his fork and spoon, and finally the extravagance of a bar of soap.

Bow and arrows and a hunting knife he already had.

With everything in place, he felt himself properly outfitted for the trail.

"Camp break at sunup tomorrow," Mr. Jones said, as he took up the reins to drive the loaded wagon back.

"Hip-hip-hooray
For Santa Fe,"

Esty sang.

Sunrise found the camp packed and ready for the trail. Esty Lang had put in his first morning's work. It was not easy, for the madre, his immediate boss, insisted upon everything being just so. When all the utensils were cleaned and dried and stowed in the cook wagon, there was no place for the cook's helper to sleep.

Beaver Jim Jones arranged to take the boy in. He himself slept on a shelf, with pulleys slung by ropes from the roof of the covered wagon. He bedded Esty down on the floor. A large fustian sack stuffed with straw served him for pallet.

The headquarters bugle sounded as Esty was washing up at the water butt. Anson Gregory, the bugler, cupped his hands and shouted:

"All out! Gather here! The captain's got a word for you."

Everyone made for the spot. The tent had been struck and roped to the wagon. The deal table remained in its place. Spreading one hand upon it, Captain Mabbitt vaulted lightly to the top.

"I'm going to call the roll," he announced. "Answer to your names. Ready, Greg?"

"Ready," his assistant replied, opening the leather-bound camp ledger.

The leader consulted a sheet of paper. "Sam Mullins," he read. "Four-hoss Conniewagon. General trade. Right?"

"Righto," the owner of the Conestoga wagon answered.

"Yankee Soule. Pack train. Eight mules. Right?"

"Seven," the muleteer corrected. "One got the heaves and I sold him."

Into Anson Gregory's ledger went the correction. The leader continued: "Emory J. Clarke. Six pack mules and the bell mare."

"Kee-rect," said the long, lanky Pennsylvanian named Clarke.

"Bert Hoyler," the captain went on. "Four

hosses; two mules. Merchandise. *Dry* goods only." He stared hard at the wagoner.

"Yeh," Hoyler answered sullenly.

"Sid Danby. Durham wagon. Six mules. Notions and general trade."

"Keno, Captain."

"Partisan Carr. Mixed pack. Four mules, four hosses. What's that?" he broke off. Gregory was holding up the ledger for his attention. "You paid in only half your entrance fee, Carr."

"I ain't got no more cash," the man said unhappily.

"Then I'd better give you back your five dollars," the captain returned. "I hate to lose you, Partisan," he added. Carr was an odd-job man who could do a little of everything.

"Couldn't I pay up in powder?" he asked.

Outside of towns, gunpowder was often used in place of money. So were flaxseed, goose down, bullets, and even hens' eggs.

"Why, certes!" Captain Mabbitt said. "Measure out, Greg."

The census was resumed. Esty counted six wagons; two of them Durhams, two Conestogas, one homemade contraption that looked as if made up mainly of barrel staves and left-over

lumber, and Mr. Jones's travel-worthy Pittsburgh. There were forty-seven mules, twenty-
five horses including the bell mare, seventeen
men, and one boy. Esty did not forget to count
himself.

The leader was speaking again. "You all
signed on to obey orders."

An uneasy rustle passed through the crowd.
These men were used to being their own bosses.

"You ain't goin' to be bothered much with
orders, not from me." Approving laughter
greeted this. "A week from now you'll elect
your own captains according to trail law. I'll be
here to listen to complaints, but don't bother
me with your personal bobberies and quarrels."
He looked about the group. "This ain't goin' to
be any picnic with lace tidies," he warned.
"Anybody that don't like the layout can come
forward and get his ten dollars back and no hard
feelin's."

Nobody moved.

"All I got to tell you, then, is to look sharp
for gopher holes and don't stray too far from the
atajo."

"What do you think of the lot?" Anson
Gregory asked his boss as they sat side by side
on the wagon seat.

Captain Mabbitt considered. "There's maybe half a dozen of 'em that's trail-wise. The rest? Greg, you've seen the buffalo-hide slippers they bend onto oxen hoofs to protect 'em from hard-baked ground."

"Yes," his assistant said.

"I reckon most of our lot is like that. They got tender feet."

"Tenderfoot" became a word of derision in Captain Mabbitt's atajo.

CHAPTER 4

Trail Politics

UNDER Gid Prouty's direction, Esty learned his trail routine. Up at first dawn. Set up the iron tripod for cooking. Gather small wood and light a fire. Fetch water from whatever spring or stream was near. Fill the kettle and the other buckets for washing up. Build up the fire. While the kettle is boiling and the cook setting out his provisions and utensils, help the men round up and bring in the grazing animals. Serve the staples: bread, salt, bacon, tea. Wash up and pack. Report back to Mr. Jones to help harness the horses and to do any odd chores.

At noon the livestock had to be turned out to

graze and brought in later. This part of it Esty liked. He had a young mule named "Whiskers" to ride in the roundup. Evening camp was hardest of all because the mules must be unpacked before being turned out. It seemed to Esty that every amateur cargador in the outfit expected him to help with the unpacking. He had no difficulty at all in going to sleep at the close of the long day.

Gray dawn and a pain in his big toe roused Esty on the fourth morning out. Mr. Jones, fully dressed, was shaking Esty's foot to waken him. Rubbing the sleep from his eyes, the boy climbed to the ground. The trapper was pointing to the eastern horizon.

There against the brightening skyline a massed black file moved. Esty had seen buffalo before, a ranging bull or a stray calf. But this was beyond anything he could have imagined.

"Get out my musket," Mr. Jones ordered, "and go and wake the madre."

Esty dashed over to the cooking wagon and hammered on the canvas side. "Get up!" he shouted. "Come out and look."

Gid Prouty's sleepy face appeared. "I'll tan your hide," he began, "if you—" He caught sight of the black line in the distance. "Yow-ee!"

he yelled in a voice to wake every sleeper. "Prairie beef! All up."

There was a frantic hustle for guns, powder, and ball. Many did not wait to dress. They ran for their horses. About to hunt up Whiskers, his young mule, Esty was accosted by Anson Gregory, who was quite unexcited.

"Hold your horses, young fellow," he said. "That parade will be going on for a couple of hours yet."

"How many are there?" Esty gasped.

"Four or five thousand. Maybe eight or ten. They're changing their grazing grounds."

Esty started back to the Pittsburgh wagon to get his bow, but decided that it would be no good against such huge game. He changed his course, caught Whiskers, saddled him and joined the madre, Emory Clarke, Mr. Jones, and Mr. Gregory. Before they had covered the mile to the high ground, they heard the crack of the muskets. The slaughter had begun.

Esty had pictured buffalo hunting as full of

daring and danger. But there was no fight in the buffaloes. They were stupid, defenseless, helpless. The men rode up to them and fired point-blank into them. Some plunged on, bleeding. Others dropped and were trampled by the rushing mass behind. One animal, wounded, might rush blindly across the prairie only to be ridden down by three or four hunters. Esty could see neither fun nor sport in that.

Foremost in the slaughter was Bert Hoyler, candidate for trail master. He was enjoying every minute of it. When his bullets gave out, he rode along the flank of the herd, bashing at the necks of the unresisting creatures with his hatchet.

When it was all over, Esty counted seventeen buffaloes on the ground, dead or dying. Hoyler cantered up.

"There's plenty meat for you, Cookee."

"Too much," the madre replied. "There's no luck in killin' for the fun of killin'."

Hoyler noticed Esty's strained face. "What's the matter, sprat?" he jeered. "Don't like it?"

"No," Esty said shortly.

"That's because you got white spots on your liver," the other said. "I got a cure for that."

"What's that, Hoyler?" Gregory asked.

"Trail milk," the other said. He dismounted, whipped out his skinning knife, cut the throat of the dying bullock, and filled the tin cup with the blood. "Try it," he said, holding out the cup to the boy. "You'll never be a man till you're blooded."

Esty turned pale. Hoyler guffawed. "Ittle boy sicky?" he jeered. "Watch here." He emptied the cup at a gulp.

The "ittle boy" *was* sick; so sick that he had to cling to the mule's neck to keep from falling off. As soon as he was able, he turned his mount and made for the camp, followed by hoots and laughter. He was a shamed boy as he fed the fire and got ready for the delayed breakfast.

All that day he was subjected to side remarks. Hoyler nicknamed him White-liver, which was shortened to Whitey, as the others took it up. The worst of it was that he had disappointed his two good friends, Mr. Jones and the madre. They did not join in the rough banter, but he could feel their disapproval. What did they expect him to do? A thirteen-year-old boy could not fight a two-hundred-pound man.

Somehow he must recover the respect and confidence of his friends. When his chance did come, it was far from his wildest fancy.

* * * * *

The busiest man on the trail, Esty noticed, was big Bert Hoyler. As soon as the wagons rolled, he was on his rounds. He had a big white riding mule which was always abreast of some wagon or of another rider while Hoyler talked and argued. Esty asked Gid Prouty about it.

"Oh, he's parmateerin'," the cook said.

"What's parmateering?" the boy inquired.

"Politickin' for votes. He wants to rig the election for hisself and that pard of his, Three-card Smith. He's promisin' that if we vote his way, everything will be sweet and easy. To hear him tell it, we'll travel slow, eat fat, sleep soft, and lie late of mornings. That's no way to run an atajo," he said in disgust.

"Who'll you vote for?" Esty asked.

"Emory Clarke for trail master; Beaver Jim Jones for camp captain," was the prompt reply. "And you'd better do the same."

One pipe of tobacco was the usual allowance after supper. Then everybody turned in. They were too tired at the end of the long day's trail for anything but sleep.

On this seventh evening out, however, nobody left the circle around the cooking fire which Esty doused with a pail of water. Captain

Mabbitt stood up and looked about the circle with those fiercely crossed gray eyes that seemed to be always out of focus, yet to take in everything.

"Everybody here?" he asked.

"All present and accounted for," Anson Gregory reported, as if at a lodge meeting.

"You all know why this powwow is called," the leader continued. "We're pickin' a camp captain and a trail master. The trail master is the boss of travel. As long as we're on the move, his say-so goes. As soon as we stop, the camp captain takes over. He's responsible for picking the camp sites and seein' that they're comfortable and safe."

Yankee Soule spoke up. "S'posen we don't like 'em after we've picked 'em? We might get a lazy doodle or a no-good jobbernow or a slick-and-slippery wily-pie. What then?"

Captain Mabbitt's lips twitched. "By trail law," he said, "any member can call for another election after two weeks. Now, are you ready? Speak your mind. Names!"

Bert Hoyler was jabbing Gee-haw Johnson in the ribs. The ex-ox driver lumbered to his feet. "Move for Three-card Smith for camp captain," he said.

Gid Prouty jumped up. "Move an amendment."

"What's your amendment, Gid?" Captain Mabbitt asked.

"My amendment is Emory J. Clarke. He knows a cottonwood from a locoweed. That's more than some folks around here does," he added with a mean look at Smith.

Ab Voorhees, a fat and solemn young man, nominated Bert Hoyler for trail master. Yankee Soule amended that to Beaver Jim Jones. All nominations were seconded.

"We'll vote for trail master first," the leader announced. "Show of hands does it. Who's for Bert Hoyler? Stick 'em up, boys."

There was a strong show of hands. The leader spoke Jones's name and his supporters voted, Esty with them. As Captain Mabbitt started to count, the boy's wrist was seized and his arm so sharply wrenched down that he cried out in pain. Hoyler's gruff voice behind him said:

"Boss, you goin' to let this young white-liver vote?"

"He belongs to the atajo," the leader said doubtfully.

"Does he? Has he paid in his ten dollars?" the objector asked shrewdly.

"Well, no, he hasn't," the captain admitted.

"Then he's nothin' but a yellow-bellied dish-washer," Hoyler said triumphantly. "He's got no vote. Trail law."

Reluctantly Captain Mabbitt agreed. He was a fair man. Hoyler growled in Esty's ear:

"You keep that hand in your pocket, you little ingler, or I'll twist it off your arm."

Before the buffalo hunt, Esty was sure, either Mr. Jones or the madre would have come to his aid. Neither made a move now. Esty slunk off.

If there had been any way to get back to Franklin, he would have taken it then and there.

The hands were counted. Bert Hoyler won by three votes. The choice for camp captain was closer. Three-card Smith had a margin of only one vote over Clarke. Captain Mabbitt announced the result.

He addressed the two successful candidates. "You, Hoyler, and you, Smith, you're duly elected by this atajo. Remember this: I'm back of you. The rest of you men," he continued grimly, "I got one word for you. You've had it easy so far. It ain't going to last. That's a big country out there, and—" He let his voice drop to a tone of confidential information, "it's full of fool-killers. Meeting adjourned."

The gathering dissolved in thoughtful silence.

> *"We're on our way*
> *To Santa Fe*
> *And makin' twenty miles a day,"*

sang Yankee Soule, who was of a musical turn.

Twenty miles was a slight exaggeration, but they would probably make Council Grove in three weeks of travel. Beyond Council Grove was the wilderness.

Everything had favored the Mabbitt party
thus far. The weather was fair. The animals
found the prairie grass good. The country was
cut across by many streams, large and small.
Where there was water there was sure to be
wood for the madre's cooking fires, game birds
for the shooting, and very likely deer. Gid
Prouty did not share in the general good spirits.
He had a low opinion of the newly elected camp
captain and a lower one of the trail master.

Neither knew his job, the madre said. The
atajo was being run like a church sewing bee—
no order; no discipline. They were falling behind schedule every day.

"Something's going to blow up," the madre
confided to his helper.

"Won't Captain Mabbitt do something about
it?" the boy asked.

"Give him time. He'll let 'em make their own
mistakes. Then he'll jump. That's the Old
Man's way."

The bright weather held. Going down into
Black Jack Creek, Wash Carnahan's spare-parts
wagon dished a wheel and had to be unloaded.
While repairs were being made, the men scattered to shoot wild pigeon and sage hens. Three
hours were lost. They did not make the Kansas

River that day, but camped on a grassy rise near a rivulet so small that it barely supplied water for the animals.

Toward sundown Captain Mabbitt came out from his wagon where, as usual, he had been studying his map and keeping a ledger on his supplies. He looked at the sun, which was shrouded in mist. He put his forefinger in his mouth and held it up to the wind, which had turned gusty. Walking over to the small tents under which the muleteers slept, he looked over the pegs and guy ropes. What he saw did not satisfy him, if one could judge from his frown. He returned to his wagon and summoned Anson Gregory. A few words were exchanged, and the assistant went to find Three-card Smith.

"What about putting in a pick-and-spade call?" he said to the gambler.

Smith scratched his head. "What's that mean?" he asked.

Gregory stared at him. "And you're the camp captain!" he said. "It means rain; that's what it means. It means ditching around your tents so your packs won't get soaked."

The camp captain studied the darkening sky. "But I don't see no rain clouds," he said obstinately.

"All right! All right!" the other returned. "Have it your own way."

Smith hesitated. "If it's Captain Mabbitt's orders," he began.

"It's not an order. He's giving you advice. Take it or leave it."

"I'll tell the men," Smith said, "and they can do as they like."

Most of them, it proved, liked to go to bed. The wagonmen had nothing to worry about: their trade was safe from storm within the stout-roofed vehicles. The tent dwellers were the ones whose goods were in danger. Yankee Soule, Emory Clarke and a couple of others got out their tools and cut foot-deep ditches around their tents to drain off any water that might fall. It was hard work. Their lanterns were still burning when the rest of the camp was comfortably asleep. They dragged their goods under cover and turned in.

A rumble of midnight thunder roused the sleepers. They tumbled out with shouts and curses, frantically scrabbling for their picks and spades. A violent blast of wind blew out their lanterns. The rain came in sheets, soaking them to the skin. Water dribbled into their tents and soaked the valuable trade cloth in the packs.

There was but one thing to do when the storm was over in the morning. Every wet pack must be undone and the goods spread in the sun to dry. Otherwise they would mildew and spoil. That meant a three-hour wait.

Captain Mabbitt made the rounds, inspecting the drying stuff. Still he said nothing. The men responsible for the delay would have been more comfortable if he had spoken his mind.

CHAPTER 5
The Cibola Man

RIGHT along here somewhere," Beaver Jim Jones told Esty, "the trail forks north."

The caravan was still in the grasslands. Here and there were patches of woodland; cottonwood, black locust, and, where the watercourses ran, willow and alder. The trapper handed the reins to his companion and jumped to the ground.

"Reckon I'll prospect this bit on foot," he said and trotted ahead.

Esty drove on, skirting a thicket. On the far side of it Mr. Jones was standing beside a square board nailed to a standard. Rough lettering read:

"It's a long year since I came this way," Mr. Jones said. "Up yonder—" He broke off, cupping his hand to his ear.

Esty heard it then, the unmistakable tunka-tunka-tunk of bells. The trapper ran to his wagon, seized his musket, and primed it from his powder horn. He motioned Esty to silence and stood ready.

From a narrow opening in the heavy growth, a man emerged. He was leading two pack mules. Around the neck of the lead mule hung a thong with three ox bells. The animals were unbelievably shaggy. The man was even more so. Upon sighting the wagon, he flung up his hand, palm out, in the peace gesture.

Mr. Jones put his musket back in the wagon. "Howdy, stranger," he said.

"Howdy," the man returned.

"Where's the rest of your outfit?"

"Ain't none," the man said placidly.

"What! You're alone?"

"Got my two mules," the man said.

"Well, dotch *me*! How long you been out here?"

"Ten years or so."

"Well, this has got me licked!" the trapper exclaimed. "Hitch your beasts on behind and come up."

They made room for him on the high seat. The stranger answered questions willingly enough. Beaver? Yes, there was plenty beaver up the Arkansas. Otter, too. And bears. Grizzlies. All over the place. He'd counted more than three hundred one day.

"What do you do when you meet one?" Esty asked, bug-eyed with interest.

"Speak to him kind and polite," the man said.

"You *talk* to a bear?"

"Certes. Talk to him folksy. You yell at a grizzly, and his feelin's is likely to get hurted. Then he can be mean."

Before Esty could ask more advice, Mr. Jones had taken over the questioning. Didn't the stranger have any trouble with the Indians? No, was the answer; Indians were all right if you knew how to treat 'em. You smoked with 'em. Then you palavered with 'em. Then you traded with 'em. That's all there was to it.

At the evening stop Captain Mabbitt came

over. "You must be Cibola Hatch," he said to the stranger and held out his hand.

"That's me," said the stranger, pleased. "Howdy!"

"Found any of those lost cities yet?"

"No. But I will. Gimme time."

Over the campfire that evening he talked to an absorbed circle about the Lost Cities of Cibola. Seven of them there were, out somewhere in the desert beyond Cimarron Crossing. They had been founded hundreds of years earlier by a Portuguese bishop who was also a soldier and an explorer. He conquered and converted the Indians and built the splendid cities. The houses were roofed with silver and shuttered with gold. Precious stones were set into the doorposts.

The members of the atajo kept their guest up half the night eagerly drinking in his words. The greediest listener of the lot was Bert Hoyler.

Before bidding them good-by in the morning, Cibola Hatch showed them a trail message which he had found fastened to a tree a few miles west of where he had met them. It was a rough drawing on a strip of bark, an Indian's head with feathers, and a pipe below it. Captain Mabbitt studied it.

"Indians ahead," he interpreted. "Kiotos or Osages likely. Friendly, anyhow."

"How d'you figure that, boss?" Yankee Soule asked.

"The pipe. It would be an arrow if they were on the warpath."

"Did the Injuns leave it?" Partisan Carr asked.

"No. That's white man's work. There must have been some trappers or prospectors along this way within a month or so. That bark ain't weathered much. See; here's their mark, a couple of *x*'s. Wasn't educated up to writin', I reckon. This is just as good."

Gid Prouty addressed the newly elected camp captain ."What you goin' to do about it, Three-card?"

"I dunno," Smith answered, uneasily conscious of his ignorance. "What d'you reckon I'd oughta do?"

"In Injun country you generally put out sentries around the camp," the madre said.

"Didn't you hear the Cap say these were *friendly* Injuns?" Hoyler growled.

But Three-card rather liked the idea of sentries. It gave him a chance to show his authority. As soon as the trail master gave him the "take

over" order, he asked Anson Gregory to make
out a list.

"You and the Cap don't have to do sentry-go,"
he said.

"Every man in this atajo takes his turn," the
leader's assistant said positively.

He shuffled the names in a hat and drew them
out one by one. The watches were divided up,
four men each. Every name in the outfit was
called but one. That was Esty Lang's.

He knew why. He was nobody in that atajo;
"Whitey," a coward who had failed to meet the
brutal test of the buffalo's blood. The knowledge sickened him at first, then made him bit-
terly angry. Give him his chance and he'd show
them!

CHAPTER 6

The Test

APPROACHING One-Hundred-and-Ten-Mile Creek, two days later, they sighted the Indian band. It was forty strong including squaws and papooses. Their chief made the sign of peace and rode forward. He was an Osage and his name was Chief Good Walker. As trail master, Bert Hoyler trotted out to meet him.

The Osage wanted none of him. Wasn't this Chief Salt Lick's atajo? Very well, then; he would do business with the leader and nobody else. Fetch out Chief Salt Lick.

With a sour face, Hoyler gave way. The two chiefs met and exchanged salutes.

"Para swap?" the Indian inquired.

"Para swap," the white man confirmed.

This mixture of correct Spanish and Yankee slang meant that both sides were ready to trade. The wagons formed up into a rough-and-ready market place. Packs were unrolled. Goods were spread out. Braves and squaws swarmed in, fingering everything.

The redskins had very little to offer. Their beaver pelts were poor and mangy. The buffalo hides were not worth carrying. The bird plumes were wilted and dull. Though the tribe was too far east to have any desert jewels of their own mining, they might have traded with tribes further west. To all inquiries for "bright stones," however, they presented blank faces.

It was Esty's first experience of trail trade, and it did not look promising. He found himself dealing with a young buck of twenty or so and his squaw. Though he brought out only his cheapest trinkets, they were eager for them. Nothing that they offered in return was worth the room to store it.

No para swap? It was looking very much that way when Esty had an idea. He opened his mouth, pointed to the inside of it, and champed his teeth. The young brave's eyes lighted up. He grunted at the squaw who trotted back to

the Indian lines and returned with a handsomely woven osier basket. In it were some of
the foodstuffs which the expedition was short
of: dried pumpkin, beans, and well-prepared
maize. Esty got two dollars' worth of the food
and the basket into the bargain, for beads and
buttons that had not cost a quarter.

Para swap, indeed! Esty was thinking highly
of himself as a trader. He was the lad to handle
Indians! They couldn't teach him anything
about the swap game. Trader Lang! His mood
of self-approval lasted until he went back to the
madre to brag a little.

Gid grinned and pointed to Esty's belt. The
small leather bag dangling there yawned open.
The drawstring had been cut. While he was
haggling with the brave, the squaw had per-
formed a light-fingered operation at his back.
He figured that she had got away with at least
three dollars' worth of plunder.

Trader Lang decided that he still had something to learn about para swap.

On Captain Mabbitt's map there were three
Little Cow Creeks, besides a Cow Creek and a
Bull Branch. The little cow after which this
overnight stop was named must have been, Esty

thought, a good picker. It was a pleasant spot. Camp was pitched in a shady grove beside a deep, clear pool. In spite of his unhappiness over the slur of being thought unfit for sentry duty, Esty slept soundly.

Getting the breakfast fire going was his start of the day. The first gray of dawn was forecasting dull weather when the boy stumbled across the grass to the cooking space. He had gathered dead branches the night before. With his skinning knife he whittled off some splinters which he built into a tiny pyramid. From one pocket he brought out a bit of paper; from another, his firebox. The paper was no larger than an envelope, for paper of any kind was a valuable article, not to be wasted.

The firebox, not more than eight inches long, enclosed a chunk of flint, a few strands of dried moss, and was equipped with a rough-edged steel wheel. Twirling the wheel, Esty struck sparks from the flint. One of them ignited the moss. It flared. He lighted the paper, which he had twisted into a spill and, carefully shielding it from the morning breeze, tucked it beneath the splinters. They caught. He fed the flame with twigs, then with boughs. In three minutes he had a satisfactory fire going.

Water next. Slinging four buckets on a pole, he climbed down to the pool. A swimming otter caught his eye. Dropping his burden, he followed it stealthily downstream past a riffle and up an overhanging bank through which a small brook cut. At the top was an open space among low trees. There he saw the remains of a man-built fire.

This was surprising enough. What astonished him more was the presence of a dozen bark plates and a tin cup. White men had been there and had left in a hurry. A trailsman was no more likely to abandon his cup than his knife. There had been danger of some sort in that place.

Esty gave a shout that woke the sleeping encampment. In three minutes he was surrounded by fellow members wanting to know what was up. They prowled among the ashes and cast about for further indications.

"Injuns musta run 'em out," Gee-haw Johnson said nervously, and looked over his shoulder.

Beaver Jim Jones had been examining the ground. "Don't reckon so," he said. "No signs of a fight. Injuns wouldn't have left the cup, either."

Shouts came from a thicket which several of the men were exploring.

"I saw it first." "Finders keepers. Them pants is mine." "Who'll give a shilling for the cap?" "Look-it! Here's a shoe!"

They came out, squabbling good-humoredly over an assortment of clothing. Hoyler was struggling into a leather jacket. Wright hugged a pair of serviceable pants close to his chest. Others passed a woollen cap from hand to hand.

"Drop that stuff, you fools!" Captain Mabbitt's voice from the edge of the clearing meant precisely what it said. One by one the garments fell to the ground.

Captain Mabbitt strode around the clearing, pushing into the thicket at points. His last foray took him to the high riverbank. He beckoned and pointed down to a wooden board, fixed in the sand, above high watermark. Nobody had to ask what it was.

The leader let himself down through the loose rubble, followed by the others. He peered at the headboard. The lettering was partly defaced by weather. He read:

"Chri—that's Christopher, I reckon—Hark—looks like Harkness—Died June 16, 1822—of—What's this?—Oh, yes!—of the Great Epidemy."

"My God!" a trembling voice said. "Smallpox!"

Captain Mabbitt took off his cap. The others did the same. He said a brief prayer.

"Back to camp everybody," he ordered. "I call a trail meeting."

They formed a crescent around Captain Mabbitt's Conestoga wagon. He brought from the inside the metal box by which he set such store, and put it on the seat beside him.

"The place we have just left," he said, "may be poisoned with smallpox. The dead man's clothes surely are. Do you know what this is?" He held up the box. No immediate reply being heard, he answered himself. "It's kine-pox; genuine kine-pox. If anything can save you from the epidemy, this is it. I scratch a little place on your arm and rub it in. That's all there is to it. It's called vaccination. Now, then, who's for it?"

Hoyler, Voorhees, Smith, Gee-haw Johnson and several others huddled together and muttered. Johnson was thrust forward. He began in a whimpering voice:

"Ain't no trail law to make a man take cow poison into hisself."

The leader cut him short. "You're right, there. I'm not giving an order." A sigh went through the gathering. "But I'm telling you this." The ludicrously crossed eyes snapped.

The voice crackled. "Anybody that don't get vaccinated and that shows one spot—just one—he gets put out of this atajo at the point of my knife, and he stays out at the muzzle of my gun. He'll sicken and he'll die alone in the empty land."

The members looked at one another, aghast. Now they were terrorized either way. The leader's grim gaze swept them.

"Are you men or are you sheep?" he rasped. "Step up, somebody! Beaver Jim, you've got the name of a brave man."

Silently Mr. Jones took off his coat, rolled up his sleeve and exhibited the circle of scar on his long-muscled arm. Emory Clarke, Anson Gregory, and Sam Mullins followed suit.

"All right," Captain Mabbitt said impatiently. "You're safe. What about you, Hoyler? You had on the dead man's coat." He took a stone in his hand and began to whet his knife. Wheep-wheep! It was a shivery sound.

Hoyler turned a sickly pale. He hung back. "I—I ain't feelin' just right," he quavered.

"Wants somebody to give him a lead," Captain Mabbitt said. His eyes swept the cringing group. "Well! Come on!" he continued impatiently. "Somebody's got to be a hero."

It seemed to Esty that the speaker's strange eyes were directed at him. He did not want to be a hero. How could he be when his knees were wobbling? He staggered forward into the open space.

"You?" Captain Mabbitt said. His voice sounded surprised, amused, and Esty thought, kindly.

"Y-y-y-yes, sir," he said.

"Roll up your sleeve . . . Higher . . . That'll do. Steady now."

Crisscross the keen knife slashed. Esty shut his eyes as the best defense against dizziness. The arm was seized, squeezed, something rubbed into it, and a bandage bound on. He did not realize that it was all over until he felt a friendly slap on the flank and heard the vaccinator's voice crying jovially: "Vaya!"

He "vaya'd" with a relieved and thankful heart.

"Next!" called the operator.

Ready hands thrust Bert Hoyler forward. He bared his arm with the expression of a man facing the gallows. At the first burning touch of the knife edge, he flopped over in a dead faint. The vaccinator had to get down on all fours to finish the job. When he rose, he remarked:

"I don't reckon we'll hear anything more about white livers from *him*."

That evening after supper the camp captain read the orders for the night.

"Third watch, three to six A.M., Johnson, Danby, Carr, and Lang."

"And Lang." Esty thought they were the pleasantest words he had ever heard in his life.

CHAPTER 7

Bad Luck Day

"SOME DAYS," Gid said philosophically, "everything goes boggledy-botch without half tryin'. This is goin' to be one of 'em."

The start was bad. The camp had been pitched near a shallow pond where mosquitoes and deer flies bred. The mosquitoes worked on the men all night, and the flies started in on the stock at sunrise. Two of Sid Danby's mules got into a fight, and Sid was badly bitten trying to separate them. Two others found a patch of loco plant and under the intoxicating influence of the crazyweed went out to dance in the moonlight. Wash Carnahan's horses were in such a hurry to get away from the tormenting flies that they bolted and upset the patchwork wagon.

By the time the repairs were made, Sid Danby's wounds dressed and the mules sobered up, an important member of the atajo had disappeared. The white bell mare was missing. As a good hour had already been wasted, Bert Hoyler gave the word to hit the trail. Let the fool whiteface find her own way, he said.

"Why, the dummed zany!" was Gid Prouty's comment when the order reached him. "No mule train will travel without a bell mare to lead. Hoyler'd ought to know that."

"Why won't they?" Esty asked.

"That's the way mules is. Look at 'em now, stretchin' their necks to see where she is."

"You mean they won't start?"

"Oh, I guess they'll start all right," Gid replied. "Then you know what'll happen?" Without waiting for an answer to his question, he went on: "We'll get out on the prairie a piece— say four-five miles—and one of Gee-haw Johnson's mulas will stick his big ears up and say, 'Hey! Where's Filopena?' And a mula in the Voorhees pack'll wiggle *his* ears and say, 'How do I know?' Then the Johnson mule'll say, 'Well, I don't go another step till I find out.'

Then the whole atajo will plant their front feet and decide to stay right there till mules' judgment day."

It happened much as Gid Prouty had foretold, only worse. Not only did all the mules balk, but several of them lay down and rolled their packs off their backs.

Horsemen cast back, spreading over the prairie. They found the runaway mare, belly-deep in a creek, cooling herself and admiring the scenery. They led her back to camp. At sight of her, several other mules were so overjoyed that they rolled and bucked *their* packs off. Four ran away. Nearly three hours were lost before the packs were restored and the stray animals rounded up. Everyone was in bad humor when the noonday halt was called.

Clouds had gathered. Esty had not got the dinner fire fairly lighted when a swift downpour doused it. The madre and he could not get the wet wood to ignite. Gid summoned the others, who had run for cover, in an angry bellow:

"Cold vittles and like it!" he shouted.

It was a dripping and depressed caravan that took the trail under a drizzling sky. The noon stop had been cut short because there was a stretch of poor country between them and Fish

Creek. They needed to make the creek by nightfall.

It was almost dark when they heard the rush of the water. As camp captain, Three-card Smith called the halt. The rain was falling steadily. They would have to ditch.

"Spades out!" he shouted.

Anson Gregory ran over to him. "You're not going to camp here!" he exclaimed.

"Why not?"

"Listen to that water. That's why not. Nobody but a tenderfoot camps on the near side of a creek."

"There'll be no crossing in the morning," Emory Clarke said in support.

"There'll be no crossin' tonight. Not for me," Bert Hoyler growled. "Think I want to get drownded in the dark?"

Others backed him up. They were tired out. The animals were tired out. It was too much of a risk. Who did Gregory think he was, to give *them* orders? or Clarke either? They wanted supper and bed and they wanted it now! Morning would be time enough to cross.

Gregory turned his back on them. A moment later a shout arose. Captain Mabbitt's wagon was easing down the steep bank to the stream bed. It plunged into the swift current. Mr. Jones's quiet voice spoke in Esty's ear.

"Up, boy! We're going over."

Halfway across, Esty felt the wagon floor press upward. Mr. Jones was shouting encouragement to his horses. Two of them, Esty thought, were swimming. The current was carrying them now. Crunch! The off-wheels were on bottom. The gallant horses had recovered foothold. The wheels rolled again. They were safely over.

A wild yell from the bank they had just
quitted brought Esty's head around. Hoyler's
crowd were dancing on the shore and shouting
threats to Gid Prouty, whose wagon was already
in the water. What about supper?

"If you want your evenin's prog, come and
get it," Gid shouted back derisively.

Yankee Soule's mules were in the water now,
and so were Partisan Carr's. Sam Mullins had
found a sandbank downstream for a better

crossing. Wash Carnahan followed him. It seemed to Esty that the stream was full of struggling animals and wagons half afloat. Four mules lost their footing and were swept downstream. A rescue party of the men already across formed a chain at a sandy point and dragged them to safety. Not a man nor an animal was lost.

In the falling darkness, Esty could count but four outfits remaining opposite, Bert Hoyler, Ab Voorhees, Perley Wright, and Three-card Smith. The Hoyler faction had lost several supporters.

In the morning the rain was over, but a mighty flood thundered between the banks. As Gid Prouty put it, the highest chariot in Pharaoh's army couldn't have made the crossing.

"Will Captain Mabbitt go on and leave them?" Esty asked.

"Oh, they'll catch up with us soon enough," the madre answered easily. "The flood'll be down by tomorrow."

Everything in the packs had to be laid out and sun-dried. It was after ten when the atajo was ready to take the trail. A man was standing knee-deep near the opposite bank, signaling with a trade bandanna. It was Bert Hoyler. Captain Mabbitt went out on a sandspit and cupped his hand to his ear.

"What'll we do? What'll we *do?*" Hoyler yelled despairingly.

"Can you hear me?" the leader called back.

"Yes."

Captain Mabbitt gave him the popular advice of the day. "Go sandpaper your nose!" he bellowed and turned his back.

CHAPTER 8

The Jumping-Off Place

COUNCIL GROVE was the real jumping-off place for the wilds. The first fixed spot beyond was Pawnee Rock, one hundred and forty-three miles across the trailless prairie. Half as far again beyond that the Arkansas River divided the United States from Mexico. The local storekeeper said darkly that they'd be lucky if they hung onto their scalps that long. The Indians out there, he said, had a notion that the country belonged to them. They didn't like white men coming in. Captain Mabbitt had better have plenty of powder and ball.

A halt of three days was called for general repairs. The first business for the atajo was a trail meeting. Captain Mabbitt made the announcement.

"Our trail master, as you might say, has resigned." His eyes twinkled. "Leastways, we got no trail master. Likewise our camp captain. We'll elect new ones."

Emory Clarke was nominated for camp captain and Beaver Jim Jones for trail master. No other names were put up. Anson Gregory called the roll. Esty Lang heard with a thrill of pride his name called. Nobody objected this time. He had a vote. He was a full-fledged member of the atajo.

"Don't get too cock-a-hoop over it, though," the madre warned him. "Easy days is over. Beaver Jim ain't no Bert Hoyler, nor Emory J. Clarke a Three-card Smith. This atajo is goin' to school."

At sundown of the second day the men who had stayed on the wrong side of Fish Creek straggled into camp. They were battered and weary. Two of their mules had been lost in the flood. Neither Hoyler nor Smith had the spunk to protest when they learned that their jobs had been given to better men.

A new discipline set in with the departure

from Council Grove. Beaver Jim Jones made the announcement over the breakfast fire.

"This atajo is goin' to be run trail fashion from now on. We're an army. We're goin' to march in order and camp in order—that's Emory Clarke's lookout—and fight in order if we have to fight. We start now. The first outfit that's packed for the trail gets the head of the line. Get to your places and wait for the word." He gave them one minute leeway, then shouted, "Ready?"

The men liked this. It was a game, a contest. The excited answers came back from all sides. "Ready." "Ready here." "Give us the word."

Trail Master Jones raised both hands above his head. Down they came with a sweep.

"Catch up!" he shouted.

At the signal, a frantic race began. Every wagon crew, every pair of mule drivers hustled for the honor of being first. Mules were packed and cinched tight. Wagons were loaded, the horses harnessed and hitched in. There was a mighty bustle and confusion. When it was at its height a triumphant voice shouted:

"All set!"

"Madre's wagon wins," the trail master announced. "Go to the head, Gid."

As the cook wagon moved proudly forward, other cries arose. "All set," from Yankee Soule's mule outfit. "All set there," from Doggo McIntyre and Perley Wright in the same breath.

The trail master waited until the last call. "Fall in," he ordered.

The wagons settled into single file. The mules and the horses jostled uncertainly for places. It was an uneven and uncertain line. Beaver Jim Jones rode along it, coaxing and prodding it into some sort of order before giving the final command.

"Stretch out!"

"Hep!" the muleteers snapped. "Giddap!" the wagoners exhorted their horses. "Haw, there, haw!" Gee-haw Johnson bellowed, forgetting in the excitement that he was not managing a yoke of oxen. The cavalcade straggled out on the plain.

Four days later it had settled into military exactness. The line formed up like a company of cavalry, with the outriders taking their places without orders. The animals knew where they belonged as well as the men. Woe to the horse or mule that tried to take another's proper place. A swift kick in the ribs admonished him to behave himself.

Esty felt proud to belong to such a slick-and-smart organization.

This was all Indian country now. The Mab-bitt outfit found plenty of signs. They came upon coyotes feeding on the butchered bodies of buffalo. At both forks of the Little Arkansas dead campfires showed that bands had been there recently. Whether they belonged to hostile tribes there was no telling. The only safe way was to be ready for trouble.

Orders were given to go into corral formation for the night. The wagons formed a loose open square with the unloaded packs at the corners and the livestock tethered near. In case of alarm the animals could be driven inside the square. Attackers could be stopped by gunfire from the marksmen sheltered beneath the wagons or behind the packs.

Some of the men complained of the extra work. Bert Hoyler was their leader. He was stirring up discontent, hoping to call for a new election. He was backed by a small clique of shirkers and hang-backers: Three-card Smith, Ab Voorhees, Perley Wright and Gee-haw Johnson. Sometimes Wash Carnahan, Doggo McIntyre, and Partisan Carr hobnobbed with

them over the evening pipe. They all agreed on one point, that Beaver Jim Jones and Emory Clarke were pushing them too hard.

"A lotta dawpluckers and scrimshankers. Wait till one of 'em gets a Pawnee arrow through his gizzard," Gid Prouty said grimly. "That'll wake him up."

It was Beaver Jim Jones's policy to make as

little showing as possible. The best way to keep out of trouble was not to be seen. On the trail he took advantage of cover wherever it could be found. The outriders covered a wide territory. Orders were strict; if a human being was sighted, the rider was to gallop back at once and report. On no account was he to fire a shot, unless he was cut off. Hoyler did not think much of this either. He boasted to his pals that if he saw a loose Injun, he'd take a shot at him on general principles.

Big Cow Creek was passed. Plumb Buttes reared up out of the flat plain. Between the little hillocks and the approaching column was a small gully, thinly fringed with bushes. Partisan Carr, who was riding post on that side, disappeared into the dip. At once he came into view again, bending over his mule's neck and lashing it to its best speed. He rode straight to the leader's wagon.

Anson Gregory's bugle blew. The wagons drew in for defense. Guns were loaded and primed. A file of savages wound up out of the dip and halted. There were about forty in all, several of them squaws. War parties did not take their women with them. One look satisfied Captain Mabbitt.

"Down muskets," he ordered.

An elderly Indian rode forward from the band. Captain Mabbitt walked out to meet him. The chief made a sign with his hand. The captain responded with the same sign. Captain Mabbitt turned to his followers:

"Para swap," he said. "Get out your stuff, boys. Market's open."

Esty noted that the redskins looked well fed, prosperous and contented. They had some fine buffalo hides and some good beaver and otter. Heavy stuff, however, was not what the whites wanted at this stage. To the chief who spoke a little English, they spoke of "shiny stones." The chief admitted having a few; small ones only, for which they had traded with the desert tribes farther west. He produced some small peridots and pale turquoises.

"He's holdin' out," Gid said in Esty's ear. "They've got better stuff than that."

Esty went over to the wagon and came back with his pockets outlined in angles. Seating himself upon the ground, he drew out a jew's-harp and began to twang it. Two of the squaws pattered forward to listen. A young brave approached; then three more. Soon the player had a curious and interested audience. The circle parted as the chief approached. He had heard at Council Grove from another chief of the strange apparatus which the palefaces bit on but did not swallow.

"Tickle-tooth?" he inquired of the musician.

"Tickle-tooth," Esty replied gravely.

The chief held out his hand. The instrument was placed in it. He applied the metal to his mouth. The effect was too much for his tribal dignity. He relaxed into a series of delighted chuckles which did not improve the music. However, the player was more than satisfied.

"How much?" he asked.

"Five dollars gold," Esty said boldly.

"No gold," said the Indian.

"No swap," said the white boy.

To give up the delightful toy was beyond the Indian's powers. He fumbled inside his richly beaded shirt and brought out what to Esty looked like quill pens. But this Indian was a trader, not a writer. Each carefully stoppered quill held a small quantity of gold dust. The chief measured out a few grains upon a piece of bark. Esty shook his head. The chief added a little more—a little more still—a slow trickle, until the young trader raised his finger. An approving voice back of him said:

"That's right, boy. Always trade fair even with an Injun." It was Captain Mabbitt.

Esty disposed of four more instruments, one for a clear, pale-green "emerald," two for fairly good turquoises, and the other for a beautifully woven blanket. It was a good day's trade.

In reply to questions, the chief advised them to keep a close watch and use only alder for their cooking fires. Alder burns with a clear flame and gives off no smoke. Pawnee Rock, two days westward, was a danger spot. Near there Comanches had scalped an American a short time before.

On the other side of the Rock they would be in constant danger until they reached the Arkansas River. After that, the going would be safer.

CHAPTER 9

Halfway

PAWNEE ROCK was reached without any encounters. Several times the outposts reported Indians in the distance. These were lone riders. They might be scouts for tribes on the warpath: Pawnees or Comanches or Arapahoes.

Although it was only midafternoon when they reached the Rock, the officials decided to make camp there. The top of the height from which the plain could be viewed for miles was the safest spot. The train unpacked and formed the hollow square for defense.

There was no grazing for the animals on the heights. They must be double-hobbled and

turned out to feed on the prairie grass below.
If an Indian attack did come, the first effort
would be to stampede the animals. Sentries were
warned to be extra watchful. On the trail the
order had been not to shoot unless in self-
defense. This was changed for night patrol. Anyone seeing a prowling Indian was to shoot to
kill.

Hitherto Esty when on sentry go had been
furnished only with a whistle for signaling.
Now, on being assigned to the second watch, he
applied to the campmaster for a gun. Mr.
Clarke was doubtful.

"Would you know how to use it if you had
one?" he asked.

"Yes, sir," the boy said eagerly. "Gid Prouty
taught me."

The kindhearted madre had expended some
of his valuable ammunition giving his young
friend a lesson. Esty had successfully brought
down two crows and a buzzard and had missed
a prairie dog by only a foot or two.

"Well, you've got to begin sometime, I
reckon," Mr. Clarke said. "There's a spare fusil
in Captain Mabbitt's wagon."

Esty's station was on the brink of the cliff.
He had already loaded his flintlock, pouring the

powder down the muzzle, carefully dropping in the round lead ball, and ramming down the wadding. He set the flint. He stared out into the darkness until his eyes ached. Nothing happened. Nothing moved . . .

Yes! Something down there *was* moving. It was edging forward through the long grass. Every nerve in Esty's body was jumping. With a mighty effort he controlled his hand to loosen the powder horn from his belt. He worried out the stopper with his teeth. Some of the grains spilled over from the flashpan of the gun, but enough remained. He leveled the barrel, took steady aim and fired.

The kick knocked him flat on his back. In his
eagerness he had put in an overcharge of powder. Half-stunned, he struggled to his feet. The
corral was in an uproar. Captain Mabbitt's hand
fell on his shoulder.

"Did you get him?"

"Y-y-yes, sir; I guess so." The marksman was
still badly shaken.

"A Pawnee?"

"Yes, sir; I guess it was."

A small, curved sliver of moon came out from
behind a cloud, and a great shout of laughter
rose from the men grouped on the height. Captain Mabbitt's command rose above the racket.

"Greg! Go out and fetch in that wounded
Pawnee. And watch out he don't kick you!"

Esty had shot the right ear off Doggo McIntyre's lead mule. If there had been a hole in
Pawnee Rock, he would gladly have crawled
into it.

Something thumped him between the shoulder blades. The madre's comforting voice said:
"Never mind, lad. That was good shootin'."

Esty knew what awaited him in the morning.
At breakfast he was hailed as "Muley." "Hey,
Muley!" "Sure-shot Muley." "Turn Muley out
to grass." It was all good-humored. No mean-

ness in it; not like being called "Whitey." Nobody had called him that since the vaccination
episode.

Four days out from Pawnee Rock the rain set
in. This was more than a discomfort; it was a
danger. The travelers could not see more than
a few yards in any direction. They might run
upon a band of Indians without warning.

An anxious conference was held between the
trail master, the camp captain, and Captain
Mabbitt. It was decided to wait for clear
weather. They spent two miserable days hidden
in the sparse growth of a shallow coulee. There
was thin grazing for the animals and only cold,
uncooked food for the men. Making a fire with
wet wood was positively forbidden. The smoke,
drifting downwind, might be scented by a keen
nose miles away.

Shortly after noon of the third day, the rain
stopped. The clouds lifted upon a scene that
gave the travelers a worse chill than the coldest
rain.

Against the skyline moved a long file of
mounted men. Some carried long lances with
bright pennons fluttering from the tips, a sign
that this was a war party. Captain Mabbitt

thought that they were Apaches, one of the most
dreaded tribes noted for their ferocity and courage. They were not half a mile away.

The leader issued his low-voiced orders. The
men must, above all, keep out of sight. If they
were discovered, nothing could save them, for
there were more than three hundred savages in
that moving line. Nevertheless, they would
make a fight of it.

Six of the best shots were stationed in the
scrub willows at the top of the bank. In case of
a charge, they were to shoot down as many
horses as possible, then fall back on the wagons
to reload while the others went forward. Esty,
and Perley Wright, who was suffering from sun
blindness, were told off to hand out powder and
ball.

The next two hours stuck in Esty's memory
as the worse strain he had ever suffered. At what
moment would there appear atop of the nearest
rise a band of whooping, yelling savages in full
charge? He tried to steady his nerves by going
over what he had to do if the attack came. Measure out the powder. Have the bullets ready in
his pocket. See that the few extra guns were
charged. Watch the marksmen for the signal.
And all the time, keep cover.

A faint yell from the distant army reached his ears. The attack was on! But it was not coming their way. Then he saw why. A herd of antelope had cut across the war party and turned it to instant pursuit. The last of the Apaches vanished at full gallop.

It had been a bad scare. For two days they lay up by day and hit the trail at night. Then the pebbly hills flattened out. The soil became spongy. Sunrise brought the welcome sight of cottonwood trees.

They pressed eagerly on, putting extra horses to the wagons when they threatened to bog down, joining up to haul straying mules from quicksands, plowing doggedly ahead, rod by rod, yard by yard.

High noon and they were at the river edge in the heat and glare of the day. The Arkansas! Halfway! Men and beasts waded into the swift, bright current and let it wash the weariness out of bone and muscle.

CHAPTER 10

The Troublemaker

THE great bend of the Arkansas River was a wilderness crossroads. As many as ten or a dozen expeditions passed that way in the course of a year. Here was the Cimarron Crossing, a safe ford to the unsafe south of the desert. Bearing to the northwest ran the known trail along the river and into the mountains.

Some of the men were for taking the short cut to Santa Fe through the unmapped desert. Their imaginations and hopes had been excited by tales of the Lost Cities and their riches. The more sober-minded objected; the region was not called the Journey of Death for nothing.

The Spaniards knew its perils. They had a

101

saying that "a bachelor wolf with no dependents could not make a living there." The main difficulty of travel was the "waterscrape," by which was meant the amount of water that could be carried to supply men and animals. In the torrid heat of that bone-dry waste, shortage of water meant death.

Captain Mabbitt said that they need not be in any hurry to decide. For ten days or so they could try the region they were in for furs. Beaver signs were plentiful. The men got out their traps and put them in order.

Esty Lang had no traps. At six dollars apiece he had not been able to afford them when buying his stock at Barney's. He did have his fishing tackle. He had only to mention fresh fish to the madre in order to get an afternoon off.

From his possible-bag he selected line and hook and cut a sliver of lead from Mr. Jones's bullet supply for a sinker. The first moist spot into which he thrust his spade yielded a supply of worms. He skirted the river for a mile and came out over a quiet pool where the current formed a backwater. It looked fishy. A dead tree lay, half submerged in the water. Esty crept out on it and cast.

Flash! The line was almost torn from his

hands. It zigzagged furiously through the surface. No catfish in the Big Muddy had ever
pulled like that. The fisherman cautiously let
himself down to a sandspit at the stream level.
There he played his catch until it was exhausted,
and he could haul it up on the sand.

Instead of the dull, oily black of the logy catfish, it gleamed with silvery scales which showed
brilliant eyespots of crimson. The delighted
angler cut a forked stick from an alder and
strung his prey on it. He rebaited, cast out his
line, and almost instantly had another heavy
strike. This one he lost through lack of skill,
and the next. He took the lead off his line and
let it float down current. This netted him two
small ones and another whopper. When it was
time to return, he had a fine string of seven.

The madre identified the catch. "Mountain
trout," he said. "That big one'll go four pound."

"Are they good to eat?" the boy asked.

"Wait till you see what the men do to 'em,"
Gid grinned.

After that first meal of trout everybody
wanted to go fishing. Esty was the only person
who had real tackle. It was a monopoly of sport-
ing goods at a place and time where they were
in hot demand. Trader Lang let it be known

that he would dispose of his surplus—at a price.

"How much?" Wash Carnahan asked.

"A skin apiece for the full outfit," the trader replied.

There was a general howl. "Why, you little ingler!" Bert Hoyler snarled. "That rig didn't cost you four bits back in Franklin."

"Well, a fella's got to make a profit, hasn't he?" the boy retorted.

Though they good-naturedly denounced him as a skinflint and a bloodsucker, the men had to admit that it was fair trade. He disposed of his whole reserve stock after lively bidding. Then, by shrewd cross trading he came into possession of what he had most needed, two beaver traps. Not only was he a trader; he would now be a trapper.

After that, the atajo never lacked for fresh fish.

Two horsemen rode up to the ford on the south side. They were well mounted and handsomely dressed in the Spanish style. The taller and older one waved his hat and shouted through his cupped hands:

"Amigos. Mexicanos."

Captain Mabbitt's knowledge was sufficient

to understand that they were Mexicans and friendly. He sent for Esty.

"Here's where you earn your pay as interpreter, young fellow," he said. "We'll go across."

They forded the stream and were greeted by the strangers. The spokesman looked Captain Mabbitt in the eye and said gravely, "Why did your man shoot at us?"

The captain looked disturbed. "What's that?" he asked sharply. "Shoot at you? Who did that?"

"A big man and heavy," the Mexican answered. "He wore a hat gay with ribbons. He fired without warning and galloped away."

No further information was needed. Bert Hoyler was notorious for his love of fancy colors. The captain's face darkened.

"Tell him it was a mistake and I am sorry," he ordered Esty.

The assurance appeared satisfactory. The two horsemen fired questions at the Americans. Where were they from? How long had they been on the trail? How did they escape the hostile Indians? Why had they come so far? What was their business?

"Para swap," Captain Mabbitt replied.

The men became excited. Both talked at once. Trade? Then the Americanos must surely go to Santa Fe. A great and rich city. Hungry for trade goods. Cloth. Iron. Paper. Tools. Anything that the so wonderfully ingenious gringoes made with their so wonderfully talented machinery.

Captain Mabbitt looked dubious. "Tell 'em," he instructed Esty, "that we'd like to go but that Santa Fe is bad medicine for Americans. The Spanish governor is a hard man and unfair. He threw the Baird-McKnight expedition into jail nine years ago, and they're still there. Tell 'em that."

Before the translation was half through, the caballeros broke in, in a frenzy of objection.

Hadn't the señor heard? Mexico had risen against Spain and declared its freedom. Santa Fe had chased out the governor, who was no good anyway, and had put in an alcalde of their own, very strong for trade. Let the Americans bring their goods to the great market place. They would go away millionaire-men.

"Good!" Captain Mabbitt said. "Tell 'em we'll be there."

The Mexicans advised against attempting the short cut across the Jornada. Better keep along the river, go up into the mountains, and then strike south. It was a wonderful fur country and a plain trail all the way. But when they saw the wagons, they were dumfounded. Never would the captain get through that region of steep cliffs and huge rocks with wheeled vehicles. He must leave his wagons and go forward with a pack train if he ever hoped to reach Santa Fe.

Captain Mabbitt thanked them politely for their advice. Watching his expression, Esty was sure that his purpose was not changed. The leader was a difficult man to convince of anything he did not want to believe.

Back in camp, the leader sent for Bert Hoyler. The big man swaggered up to the tent, trying to look undisturbed. Captain Mabbitt said:

"Hoyler, did you shoot at those Mexicans?"

"Well, I kinda fired a charge in their direction."

"What for?"

"I took 'em for Injuns."

"That's no reason. You heard the orders not to shoot except in self-defense."

"That was on trail," Hoyler returned sullenly. "We ain't on trail now."

Captain Mabbitt deliberated. When he spoke, it was slowly and quietly. "Hoyler, you've been a troublemaker since we started. Disobey another order and I'll have you flogged."

Hoyler's face turned purple. His lips drew back in a snarl. "You'll-have-me-flogged?" he said in a strangling voice.

"Before the whole atajo," was the quiet reply.

Hoyler spat on the ground. "I'm through with your blasted atajo," he said. "Gimme back my ten dollars. I quit."

"When?"

"When I get blasted good and ready."

"So do," the leader said. "We'll be well rid of you at the price."

Hoyler stamped away muttering.

After the evening meal Esty strolled down to the ford. The last rays of a blazing sunset sud-

denly were gone and the water was dark for a
moment—then dimly lighted as the evening star
was reflected on its surface. A group of three
men stood ankle-deep in the water, apparently
washing some of their gear. One was talking in a
low voice. Esty recognized him as Hoyler, whom
he thought had already left camp. They came
out of the stream when they saw him and
walked toward camp. Esty cupped his hands
and splashed water on his face. He was tired and
sleepy. Then, refreshed, he started slowly strol-
ling back. There was a sudden movement in
the bushes and a stunning crash.

CHAPTER 11

Mirage

MEMORY came back to Esty in painful throbs. He could remember stuffing himself with berry pie at supper and still feeling overfed when he walked down to the ford to wash. Nobody else was stirring. Nothing unusual about that. He was always the first one up, having the cooking fire to start. Had he built a fire that morning? Not so far as he could recall. He must have been shot as he was crossing the open space.

He was sure he had been shot, until he felt himself all over and failed to find any wound. There was, however, a sizable bump on the back of his skull. That would explain his headache.

110

Who had hit him and why? What time was it?
And what day? Where was he? Whither was he
bound in this wagon that jolted so painfully under him? The best guess he could make was that
the atajo had been attacked by Indians and that
Mr. Jones had escaped in his wagon, taking him
along. His head felt queer. He went back to
sleep. When he woke again it was dark. He
called for Mr. Jones.

A lighted lantern revealed the interior of a
wagon and Bert Hoyler's grinning face. "Alive,
huh?" he said.

"I guess so," Esty replied dully.

"That's good. You're more use to us alive
than dead."

"Could I have a drink?"

Hoyler brought him a small cupful. "Our
waterscrape ain't too much," he said. "We're on
rations till we get there."

"Where?"

"Cibola."

Quite good-humoredly for him, Hoyler explained that he, Three-card Smith, and Ab
Voorhees had decided to look for the Lost Cities
by themselves. "You're goin' along as interpreter," he said. "Sorry we had to bat you over the
head."

The scheme was plain to Esty now. The three conspirators had stolen a wagon—he recognized it as Sid Danby's Durham—stocked it, laid for him last evening, knocked him senseless, and kidnaped him.

"And if you figure on givin' us the slip," the man continued, "wait till morning, and take a look."

The morning look was not encouraging. On all sides stretched the dreary desert. Nothing grew there but cactus and a few sprangling, strong-smelling creosote bushes. Nothing lived there but the small, evil creatures of the infertile sand, centipedes and scorpions and ants. How far they were from camp and the river, the captive had no way of knowing. He did note that they were headed southwest.

He was told to turn out and get breakfast. Some dead cactus was the only fuel he could find to start his fire.

As the outfit had traveled all night, it laid up for a rest after eating. Never had Esty known anything like the blistering heat when they took up the journey shortly after noon. At the next stop Ab Voorhees rolled a keg out of the wagon and broached it. A powerful fume came from the bunghole. Esty now recalled that while they were at Cimarron Crossing, Ab and Bert Hoyler had gone out into the desert with their hatchets and brought back some maguey cactus which they had boiled up and set aside. It had fermented into the strong beer which the Mexicans call "pulque."

Under its influence his captors quarreled at supper over a map of the desert on which were dotted three of the lost cities. Esty recognized the map. It was one which the Council Grove storekeeper had tried to sell to Gid Prouty for a dollar. The madre had refused, remarking that when he needed a map to Nowhere, he'd draw it himself.

In Bert Hoyler's opinion, they were close upon one of the cities and should reach it on the following day if they kept going. The other two disagreed violently. They wrangled and fought and returned to the pulque until they staggered drunkenly off to sleep.

Here was Esty's chance. He waited until all three were snoring, then edged out of the wagon on his stomach. Cautious though he was, he jostled a hanging object which gave out a tinny sound. It was a pewter canteen which one of the sleepers had put aside. A fortunate find! He filled it and slung it to his belt, then drank

his fill from the diminishing waterscrape. Three-
card Smith's big, gray mule was hobbled near.
About to mount, Esty had another thought.

There was a reserve olla, an earthenware jar,
which one of the trio had picked up somewhere,
full of the precious water and loosely covered
with canvas. Esty rolled it out, ripped off the
cover, and invited the gray to help himself. The
amount the gray consumed made a terrific dent
in the supply. Let the others worry about that.
They had a compass, stolen from Captain Mabbitt, Esty suspected, and could probably find
their way back to the river if they had to.

How he was to find his way there was another
matter. It was somewhere to the north; that
much he knew. Fortunately he remembered
Mr. Jones had taught him how to find the North
Star. You sighted along the two stars that
formed the outer rim of the Big Dipper. Esty
did that. Sure enough, there it was. He pointed
the gray mule's nose for it, and they set out.
Sunrise found them well out of sight of the
camp.

Over that gently rolling ground, a mule
should be good for five miles an hour. For the
first few hours they did about this. Then the
hard rubble was succeeded by soft sand. The

gray struggled gamely, but its pace slowed down
to a stumbling walk. Esty dismounted. The
shifting sand gave before his feet and poured in
on top of them at each step. He could hardly
drag himself forward. He fell. It was too much
trouble to stand up again. Nearby was a bush.
He crawled into the little patch of shade cast by
it, unslung his canteen and took a pull at the
sun-heated water. The mule nuzzled at the

juiceless leaves on the bush but found them un-
eatable. It closed its eyes, hung its neck, and
stood.

Twilight was over the desert when Esty woke
up. He was bathed in sweat. A furious thirst
beset him. Again he unstoppered the canteen.
It was half-empty. Had he drunk so much already? He was terrified. He forced himself to
put the stopper back after he had filled his
mouth and held the water, unswallowed, until
the thirsty glands had absorbed it.

A brisk breeze blew across the waste. It was
discouragingly cold. Chilled to the bone, Esty
urged his mount forward. Now the ground was
firmer. They could make better time, guided by
the pale but steady light of the North Star. Up
there somewhere the great Arkansas ran swift
and clear and cool. It could not be very far now.

He took another slow swallow of the precious
water. How much was left? He shook the canteen. It gave out a hollow sound. Perhaps a cupful sloshed around in the bottom. When that
was gone—but it was better to think of something else.

"Giddap, mula!" Esty said, and the gray
wiggled its ears.

The wind rose and rose. Now it was a strong

gale. It whirled great clouds of sand high into the air. The stars were blotted out. Esty had no point of guidance. He could only blunder ahead, hoping to keep the right direction.

Alternately riding and plodding beside his weary mule, Esty got through the blind night. A sickly radiance diffused itself in the wind-driven sand. The gale subsided. The dust settled. Esty found himself staring into the eye of the rising sun. He had lost the north and been traveling due east. How long had he been going in the wrong direction? The water in the canteen was down to the last swallow.

There was but one thing to do, turn to the north and keep going. Queer things began to happen inside his mind. He plainly heard a voice which sounded like that of the friendly young Mexican, calling:

"Agua! Agua! Otro lado." ("Water! Water! The other way.")

Turning his head, he saw the bright surface of the lake. Little wavelets dappled it. It was not more than a mile away, down in the next hollow. He yanked the mule's head around and urged it forward. The mule was not interested. It balked.

Esty's brain cleared. The bitter truth came

home to him. There was no lake. It was a desert mirage. The mule knew more than he.

The withering sun climbed overhead. Esty remembered the buffalo hunt and Bert Hoyler and the blood. The thought did not make him feel sick now. He could cut the mule's throat and keep himself alive on the blood.

No; he could not bring himself to it. If the mule died first, then he would do it. If he died first, the mule could—No! That wouldn't do the mule any good. It did not seem fair. Esty decided that he was getting lightheaded again.

He got out one of the shiny stones for which he had traded and held it on the back of his tongue. He did not think that his tongue had begun to swell yet. How long could a man live after the swelling set in? Gid had told him. Three hours, he had said. Well, they could cover quite a bit of desert in three hours. Keep going, mula!

They came to a small barranca, one of those rambling depressions that cut into the desert every which way. On the low bank was a scrawny growth which Esty took for a new kind of cactus. The mule made no such mistake. It insisted on going over to nibble at the thin wands. Only then did its rider recognize the leaves as willow.

Instinct rather than reasoning told him that where willow grows there is water. He stared down into the sandy depression. Dry as a bone! Just the same, those roots must find moisture somewhere. Picking out the lowest spot of the hollow, the boy set out to paw away the sand. He kept at it until he was panting for breath and his fingers were sore. No good. Not a sign.

He climbed the bank to study the willows and estimate which way the roots ran. When he returned to the bottom, he gave a shout that almost panicked the mule. The sand at the bottom of the hole had turned a dull black. Esty whipped out his knife and attacked the place as if he meant to rip the earth apart. Water welled up.

It was not very good water. It tasted of alkali, and the first mouthful was half sand. But it was water! Esty had never tasted anything so wonderful in his life. He let it seep through his bandanna, which freed it of most of the sand, and drank his fill. Then he deepened the hole and let the mule drink.

The rest was easy. That barranca, Esty figured out, must once have been a stream. Indeed, it was a stream now, an underground stream. Streams flow into larger streams. The barranca would lead them to the Arkansas. They skirted it and in an hour sighted the line of cottonwood trees that meant the end of their quest. An hour later they were both up to their shoulders in the life-restoring current.

Esty had to beat the mule over the ears with his canteen to keep it from foundering itself on the water.

CHAPTER 12

Trap Lore

EVENING was falling when a footsore boy and an eyesore mule came into camp. There was a warm welcome for them. Over the evening fire, Esty had to tell his story and answer numberless questions. An expedition, he learned, had set out after the theft of the wagon was discovered. It had soon lost the trail and given up.

One point was definitely settled by Esty's adventure. There would be no short cut to Santa Fe. The sandstorm pointed the risk clearly. If a boy and a mule could be lost out there in the desert, so could a whole caravan. It was not necessary to take a trail vote. Not a man who

121

had heard Esty Lang's tale would have chosen to brave the Jornada del Muerto.

As for Bert Hoyler and his companions, there was an ominous shaking of heads. Maybe they would come out at one or another of the Lost Cities. Somebody grumbled that there weren't any Lost Cities; Cibola was all a fraud. Maybe they would make their way across to the Cimarron River. Or maybe they would be lost and wandering until their waterscrape gave out and then—nobody finished that supposition.

The men of the atajo talked beaver. They had had fair luck along the river and its tributary streams, but the take was running low. Plenty of fur upriver; so said Gid Prouty and Yankee Soule and Captain Mabbitt. No; they had not been up there, themselves, any of them; but they had heard about the country from earlier travelers whom they had met in St. Louis, the center of the fur trade. Beavers that weighed a hundred pounds. Otters so big they could lick a wildcat in a fair fight. Muskrats so thick you could catch 'em in scoop net.

Time to be moving. They would follow the river, Captain Mabbitt told them, up into the mountains. There they would trap until they had all the furs they could pack. From the high

land down through Taos and San Miguel to
Santa Fe was all fine country, well watered and
full of game, so it was said.

"Are we goin' to take the wagons, Cap?" the
madre asked.

"Certes, we're goin' to take 'em," the leader
replied positively.

Doggo McIntyre kissed his hand to the sur-
rounding country. "Good-by, my sweet, easy
life," he said. "We're going to wish we was back
here, many a time."

Beaver Jim Jones was another doubter. All
mountain rivers were pretty much the same, he
said. He didn't believe anything on wheels
could get through that kind of country.

"It's your atajo, boss," he said to the leader.
"If you say 'wagons,' it's wagons. But I don't
hanker for the job of trail master. You take
over."

Captain Mabbitt said, "Will you follow me?"

"Certes. My wagon'll follow where yours
leads."

"So will mine," Gid said.

"Santa Fe or bust," Emory J. Clarke pro-
claimed.

Travel was fairly easy at first. There were
long stretches of stream where they could keep

to the river bottom. Where it narrowed, they often, though not always, found gently sloping banks up which the rolling stock could be hauled. Detours had to be made where the forest growth was thick. But there were signs enough of former pack trails to guide them.

True, they were obliged four times to unload wagons, haul them up steep cliffs with ropes, overload the mules with trade goods to be carried to the top, and pack the wagons again. But they had done it before, short of Council Grove. They grumbled, of course.

Atajo men always grumble. But it was good-natured complaining.

They came around a turn on a misty morning to find themselves confronted with a pile of huge boulders which completely blocked the land passage. Overhead, heavy forest crowned the cliffs. There was no way out there. The leader scrambled halfway up for a view ahead.

"Looks like there's quite a piece of that rock to get past," he announced when he came down.

"Here's the stoppin' place for the wagons," Partisan Carr said. " 'Nothin' on wheels can tackle that stuff."

"Then we'll take the wheels off," Captain Mabbitt said cheerfully.

"Do you expect me to risk my mules' legs climbin' that mess?" Sam Mullins demanded.

The leader pointed to the deep current. "If your mules don't want to climb, they can swim." His tone changed. "Come on, hombres! We're goin' across."

Beaver Jim Jones was already at work, with a wrench, on his wheels. Wagons were unloaded. The top hamper was stripped off. The canvas was put aside. One by one, with ropes to haul and with fresh-cut saplings for levers, they sweated the wagon boxes across the cruel rocks.

After that there was the trade stuff to be transferred on the backs of suffering, straining men. Prodded and urged by shouts and curses, the mules swam their packs up the swift current. They made it, but everything was soaked.

All day the men toiled. Back and forth; back and forth, until the breath pressed against their ribs and the muscles of their legs knotted. On the far side of the barrier was a blessed strip of flat, clean sand.

"Strip packs," the leader's remorseless voice ordered.

All the wet goods were laid out to dry. Esty helped with every sinew in his body crying out. When the last soaked cloth was spread, he ducked behind an upended rock and spread himself out, soggy as the limpest piece of cotton. Sleep! That was all he wanted.

Vain hope! The madre's heavy hand yanked him to his feet. The madre's voice boomed:

"Where d'you think you are? Fire, boy, fire!"

Driftwood was plentiful. In a sort of stupor, he gathered enough and set it alight. He ate mechanically and he supposed he must have helped wash up. Anyway, he was on his pallet in the wagon without quite knowing how he got there. Sleep at last!

Back went the wheels upon the axles in the morning. Back went the wagon boxes and up went the tops. Back went the goods into the mules' side sacks and into the wagons . . . All set! Stretch out! Off they went.

And two miles farther, they came up against a jumble of rocks worse than the first. It was all to do over again.

The next few days—he never could remember how many—were a nightmare in Esty's memory. Time after time—he never could remember how often—they dismantled the wagons and put them together again. Men tumbled over rocks. Mules fell down cliffs. Wagons toppled into the water. It was all a horrid jumble of trial and failure and another trial and success, if you could call it success when you didn't care one way or the other. For that matter you didn't care whether you lived or died, you were so tired. Esty staggered about among gaunt scarecrows who gave him silly orders in hoarse whispers.

He felt a kind of fiendish delight when they came to that impossible obstacle of a rock pile which impenetrably hemmed in the deep gorge of the river. Someone said with a sort of weary satisfaction:

"The Old Man'll never make that."

"Lay off!" Captain Mabbitt ordered. Esty was asleep before his shoulders touched the gravel. He was waked up by a sharper order:

"Axes out!"

"What's up now?" asked a stupefied voice.

"Wake up and listen!" the captain snapped. "We can't get the wagons over the rock. We can't get the mules up the cliff. The water's too deep to ford. See those trees?" He pointed to the forest of pines towering eighty feet above them. "We're goin' to cut down enough of those to build a raft. We're goin' to cut saplings to pole it. We're goin' to raft every wagon, every mule, every man, and every bedotched piece of trade upstream till we ground. Come on! Up that cliff! Stir your bones, you scrimshankers, you inglers, you wamble-cropped blausers! *Move!* ! !"

They climbed the cliff. They felled the trees. They bound together the trunks with ropes. They loaded and poled upstream and unloaded and drifted downstream, and reloaded and pushed upstream again. Once the raft broke in two. Once a horse jumped off and had to be rescued. But the job was finally done, and the exhausted workers had their reward.

Beyond the shoal which was the end of their day's toil, the country opened up, broad and level and kindly.

After the hardships of the river gorge, it was a glorious relief to come out into open country. The grassy uplands were divided by the river which flowed in a gentle current. Frequent patches of woodland gave promise of game. Mountains loomed high in the west.

The atajo was in poor shape. All the wagons were badly battered. Harnesses needed replacing. One of the horses was bitten on the foreleg by a small sidewinder rattlesnake, and was too lame to be of much use. A five-day period for rest and repairs was decreed by Captain Mabbitt.

Others could rest, it appeared, but not Esty Lang. No sooner had his cooking chores been finished than the calls upon him started.

Come here—Go there—Help me with this— Fetch that. Esty could have used a dozen pairs of hands and more legs than a centipede. He did not even have time to set his two beaver traps. The five days were over. "All set." "Catch up." They were on the move again.

"Chouteau's Island lies somewhere upstream," Captain Mabbitt told them.

Beaver Jim Jones told Esty about that. A small party of Auguste Chouteau's trappers had been attacked by a band of Pawnees and driven into the river. They fought their way across to the wooded island at sunset. After an all-day battle, they drove the savages off. This was twelve years before, in 1810. It was the first time the redskins had ever faced gunfire. Now they had a few guns of their own.

It was Mr. Jones's opinion, delivered over the evening fire, that there might still be Chouteau men in the neighborhood.

"Pawnees, too?" Partisan Carr asked.

"It's a Pawnee country," Anson Gregory said. He had the official map of the atajo before him.

"Friendly or hos-style, would you say?" Gid Prouty inquired.

"With a Pawnee, you never can tell whether it's trade or raid," Emory J. Clarke said. "We'll set out pickets again."

Whatever else it might be, it was certainly a fur country. The Arkansas and its tributary streams were alive with beaver, otter, and muskrat. The company settled down to a slow pace, a mile or two a day. Spreading out in all directions, they trapped all the available waters.

Time was what Esty lacked. With so much

daily kitchen work on his hands, what chance
had he to operate his new traps to advantage?
The best places were sure to be taken up before he could get out on the river.

He took to exploring the side creeks and figuring out the haunts of the fur-bearing animals.
He would bait the powerful springs, set them
in a chosen spot, then leave the place, get out
his tackle, and go fishing. Always he caught fish.
Generally he found prey in his traps. It might
be a beaver or it might be a snarling otter which
was nearly as valuable.

After the capture of the creatures there was
the skinning, salting, and stretching of the pelts.
And, oh, it was grueling, hard work!

A bothersome question presented itself to his
mind one morning as he sat by the wagon scrap-
ing the day before's catch. He had a fair lot of
furs, beaver and otter. Muskrat he did not
bother with. Two or three hundred dollars he
reckoned as the value of the pile that over-
topped his head when he stood beside the pile
of scraped and cured pelts. *Where was he going
to put them?*

Certainly there was not going to be room for
them in the wagon already crowded with Mr.

Jones's much larger take. Miserably he asked Mr. Jones about it.

The trapper said: "The madre shot a white-tail a couple of evenings ago."

"Yes, sir."

"And you skinned it. What did you do with the hide?"

"Left it on a rock."

"It's time you learned your trade. That buckskin is in Cookee's wagon where I put it. Fetch it to me."

Esty watched while the trapper cut long bands in the green skin. He got out the pelts and folded each one with the hair side in, making a neat pile of them. This pile he bound firmly with the leather thongs and set it out in the hot sun. By sunset, the drying bands had contracted like a vise. The skins formed a mass as hard as iron, a tenth of their former size. Esty could hardly lift them to stow them away.

"There's more to trappin'," Mr. Jones remarked, "than catchin' and skinnin' your beaver."

A distant report interrupted their talk. Esty heard the madre's quiet voice, speaking outside the wagon.

"Did you hear that?"

"Gunshot," said Mr. Jones.

"A Chouteau man, you reckon?"

"Not a white man's gun."

How could Mr. Jones know that, Esty wondered. The explanation followed.

"That was a half-charge. A white man fires a full charge. An Injun is too stingy with his powder."

"Well, I don't like it," Gid Prouty said.

Neither did Esty. He lay awake a long time. There was no other shot.

CHAPTER 13

Death at the Ford

I F there was one possession which Beaver Jim
Jones prized more than his others, it was his
fine doeskin jacket. He had hammered and
pressed and pommeled the hide until it was soft
as silk. Five buttons ornamented it: a thin
nugget of gold, a circle of silver, a turquoise, a
beryl, and a fine wood agate. Every night he
brushed it, cleaned away any spots, and hung it
on its special nail.

So Esty could hardly believe his eyes when,
at the noonday stop, he saw Mr. Jones drop his
precious garment in the river and weight it
down with two stones. It was thoroughly soaked
when he brought it out again and spread it on
the face of a rock for the sun to dry. It dried as

136

stiff as a board. Captain Mabbitt, Anson Gregory, Gid Prouty and several others came over to finger it. At the next stop, those of them who wore leather gave their coats the same treatment. The madre explained it to Esty.

"It ain't very comfortable wearin'. And I don't say as it would stop a bullet. But no arrow is goin' to git very far into it."

"Do you think the Indians are after us?" the boy asked breathlessly.

"Beaver Jim wouldn't have sp'iled his fancy coat if he hadn't thought so," the madre replied, "and what Beaver Jim thinks purty gen'-ally comes out that way."

That night the first-watch sentries reported skulking figures, half-seen in the dark. They might be wolves. Or they might be human prowlers. Certainly there were human beings around, for, just before daylight, a high, shrill, long-drawn-out whirring sound was heard in the distance. Gid Prouty recognized it.

"A Pawnee whistle," he told Captain Mabbitt. "That's the way they signal. It's a war party."

The leader called a council of his most trusted men. By the light of a buffalo-tallow candle, they studied the rough map.

"We ought to be within a couple of days' travel to Chouteau's Island," the leader said.

"What's the good of that?" Emory Clarke asked.

"There might be some of the Frenchies there," the madre suggested.

"The old cottonwood breastworks might still be standin'," Beaver Jim Jones put in.

"If we can get to 'em," Anson Gregory said.

Captain Mabbitt put his stubby finger on the paper. "F-o-r-d," he spelled out. "That spells ford. If Auguste Chouteau's men could get across it, I reckon we can."

Beaver Jim Jones straightened up and stretched himself. "Let's start," he said.

"Now?" "In the dark?" "Without any rest?" several voices objected.

Captain Mabbitt rolled up the map and put it away. "Beaver Jim's right," he said. "We'll take trail. And we'll keep goin' until we get there or—" he hesitated "—or we get stopped."

Gid spoke up. "I've fit Pawnees before. It's my opinion, for what it's wuth, that they're whistlin' in their warriors, and they won't tackle us till they're up to strength, two-three hundred maybe."

"That's my idea, too," Beaver Jim said.

"Give the signal, Anse," Captain Mabbitt ordered.

The bugle notes rang through the darkness. The camp sprang to life. The outposts came in. When the atajo formed up, ten animals were missing. The Pawnees had run them off.

The expedition went forward in close formation. It kept to the river bottom. Still no Indians were seen. It was Captain Mabbitt's belief that the savages were keeping pace with them back of the high bluffs and concealed by the forest growth. Every firearm was kept loaded and ready.

Islands were plentiful in the broad reaches of the river which they were now skirting. Which one was Chouteau's Island? In the course of their all-day travel they passed several, none of which showed any signs of occupation. Evening came. They stopped for supper and to give the jaded animals a rest.

It was a short stop. The lay of the land was unfavorable for defense in case of a night attack. Weary though men and beasts were, the orders were to press forward. The wagoners took turns; one slept while another drove. With the shortage of animals in the pack train, some of the muleteers had to foot it most of the night.

When the dawn halt was called, the animals had barely enough energy to crop the rich bottomland grass. The men dropped and slept. Esty was sent about to shake and pound them before they could be roused to take any interest in breakfast.

Map in hand, Captain Mabbitt studied the horizon. Sharp peaks showed to the west. At the end of the visible lowland, the river seemingly came up against a cliff. Actually, it made a sharp curve. The curve was shown on the map, and beyond it the island of their hopes. The leader addressed his men:

"Well, hombres, it's either there or it ain't. Catch up!"

It was there. It loomed in sight when they came to the turn, a beautifully wooded oval standing high out of the current. As they rounded the side of the cliff and saw the flats broadening before them and the ripple of the shallows between mainland and island, the tired men raised a shout.

It was answered by a wild medley of yells and whoops. Out from openings in the hills, the Indians poured forth into the plain. Riding their horses at full speed, they charged down upon the atajo. Esty guessed that there must be nearly three hundred of them. A few brandished guns. The others carried longbows. He heard Captain Mabbitt's sharp order.

"Form in corral," but he did not need the command. He was trail-hardened enough to have acted on instinct. Catching Whiskers and two other animals by the halters, he urged them into the shelter of the Pittsburgh.

Another order came. "Hold your fire, men." Captain Mabbitt's voice was cool and steady.

Esty sprinkled powder on the flashpan of the spare musket. Behind him the madre advised:

"Stow it, boy. They'll break."

To Esty the plunging line looked like a wave that must engulf them. This band, however, probably remembered with respect the gunfire of Auguste Chouteau's mountain men twelve years before. At a hundred yards' distance the horsemen swerved and swept to one side, yelling like demons. A few ineffectual shots were fired by them. Ten minutes later, the other half of the band charged past. This time a wild shot hit one of the atajo's horses, stampeding several.

The battle plan of the Pawnees, it was evident, was to harass and wear down the enemy. Back and forth they charged. Each time some daring rider came a little nearer than before.

This had been going on for an hour when Captain Mabbitt came over to the Pittsburgh wagon. Beaver Jim Jones was not only a good shot; he owned a Kentucky rifle, the best firearm in the atajo.

"Think you can get one of those fellows this time, Jim?" the captain asked.

Beaver Jim stretched flat along the wagon seat, propped the end of his gun barrel and sighted along it. "Reckon so," he said.

As the attackers swooped down, the trapper settled to his aim. Several braves formed a flying group. They dashed in, discharging arrows which described long curves and rattled against the sides of the wagon. The marksman waited, waited, waited until Esty thought he was never going to fire. Then—*boom*! The full charge of powder shook the wagon.

A brave in a headdress of brilliant feathers slumped, gripping his horse's mane. He sagged to one side, plunged, and lay twitching for a moment on the ground, before stretching and stiffening. Esty had never before seen a human being killed. It made him feel queer.

The other savages made their best speed out of range. Having tested the whites with this result, they would not threaten again for a while.

Night would be the time of danger. After consulting with Beaver Jim, Emory Clarke, and Gid Prouty, the leader explained the situation to the others. To stay where they were until darkness fell would be to give every advantage to the attackers. They would be overwhelmed and slaughtered. Their one chance was to ford the river. If they could once gain the island, there was a good chance of defending it successfully.

They moved on, slowly, with the animals inside the hollow. Eight outposts, instead of the usual four, guarded the advance. They traveled afoot, with weapons at the ready. Shooting from horseback would be too uncertain. No Pawnee cared to advance within range of one of those kneeling marksmen.

Until they reached the ford, they were not molested. The redskinned army moved along with them. The test would come when they started to cross. It would be a rear guard action. The best shots would hold off the Pawnees while the wagons and animals crossed, and would then make the ford themselves, if any of them were left.

They halted opposite the island. There was a bright ripple which seemed to extend the whole

quarter-mile. It looked dangerously swift in spots. Captain Mabbitt was speaking in his quiet voice to Esty.

"Can you drive a four?"

"Yes, sir," Esty said. He had had practice with the Pittsburgh while Mr. Jones was taking his sleep.

"Take my wagon over when I give the word. We're holding the Pittsburgh here. Keep 'em breast to current as much as you can. The pack mules will be ahead of you."

"Yes, sir," Esty said. His mouth was dry. "Are you and Mr. Jones and Gid—aren't you coming?" he faltered.

The leader had already turned away. "Pick and spade!" he shouted, and the little band fell to work throwing up entrenchments.

Esty saw it all now. So long as the full force was there, the hovering savages would not risk an attack. Their time would come when the atajo took the water, leaving only a handful of picked men to cover them. Who would those be? Captain Mabbitt for certain, and Mr. Jones, and Emory J. Clarke. Probably Anson Gregory and Gid Prouty and maybe Yankee Soule. He would like to say something to Mr. Jones. But what? Esty looked at him imploringly. The trapper caught his eye and said:

"Mind that off-wheel horse, boy. He's slew-footed in water."

It was better with Gid Prouty. He gave Esty a mighty whack between the shoulders. "Don't let 'em flambergast you, spratling," he said heartily. "Meet you in the happy hunting grounds."

Captain Mabbitt's voice sounded strained and anxious. "Guns ready." There was a rattle of spades and picks. The rear guard of six crouched behind their embankment. "Ready, mulas?" The response came back from Sam Mullins, Partisan Carr, Doggo McIntyre, and the others, "All set, boss." "Ready here, Cap." "We're on our way, Frenchy Chouteau."

"Catch up!" Captain Mabbitt shouted, and Esty wondered whether he would ever again hear that order in that voice.

The water seethed and boiled around the haunches of the plunging pack animals. A moment later Esty's name was called. He gathered the reins. "Give 'em their heads," Captain Mabbitt shouted. He sent the long whip writhing out across the backs of the four. The wagon reeled as they leaped forward. Behind him Esty heard the whoops of the charging Pawnees.

There were no river marks by which he could guide his course. Upstream on the island bank stood a dead tree. It would do as a goal for want of something better. Ahead of him the pack animals struggled and floundered. Whether they were keeping to the shallowest ridge he could not know. He tried to guess the safe line from the current before him.

From the corner of his eye he could see three Indians running out on a point below him. They waded to their armpits and unslung their bows. Thump-thump! Arrows were striking the wagon top. One came winging past him, struck the off lead horse in the flank, and quivered there. With a scream the animal lost his footing. A swirl of the current caught and dragged at him. The others were drawn after him, and in a moment the wagon was afloat.

Esty yelled to the muleteers ahead. They were having troubles of their own. He felt the sweep of the water drawing the outfit in toward the point where the three Indians, dancing and capering, waited to scalp him. Luckily he was a stout swimmer. Whipping out his skinning knife, he cut loose the plunging horses, who had the good sense to strike out for the island shore.

He was about to follow them when the thought of the atajo's valuables struck him. The moneybag. And the metal box upon which Captain Mabbitt set such store. Groping beneath the seat, he found them. The bag he fastened to his belt. The box, cumbrous as it was, he thrust down inside his shirt. As he thrust himself clear of the wagon, now whirling about end for end, he felt the extra weight drag at him. On the shore he had just left there was the crackle of gunfire. The Indian charge was on.

No use to fight that current. His best chance

was to go with it, beating his way toward the end
of the island. A few arrows plopped into the
stream behind him. That danger was over. A
crosscurrent had caught the wagon and was
swinging it into midstream. How disappointed
the three bowmen waiting on the point would
be! Their yells of rage would have made him
laugh if he had had any breath left for laughter.

Forgetting for the moment the weight he carried, he turned on his back for a moment's rest.

Instantly he went under and came up strangling. Now he was dangerously near being carried past the end of the island. Turning for a final effort, he heard a shout. Doggo McIntyre was wading out from the point in which the island ended. There was the whir of a lariat, flung by a practiced hand. The loop fell near him. He grabbed it and went skittering to shore like a tired fish.

When he could stand, he found himself

alone. One glance told him why. The Pittsburgh wagon was in the river on the far side bringing back the gun fighters, and Doggo had rushed back to join the muleteers who were trying to go to the rescue. The stream opposite was swarming with mounted Indians. Two shots were fired from the wagon. Only two! Where were the other fighters?

Whiskers was on the island shore unconcernedly foraging for grass. Esty caught up a reserve rifle, hurled himself upon the mule's back, and set out back across the Arkansas. The wagon was halfway over now, but had not shaken off the savages. The mulemen, shooting from the saddle, accounted for some. A Pawnee had forced his mount to the side of the wagon and was hacking at the canvas with his tomahawk. Esty, steadying himself with his knees, shot him through the shoulder. He dropped into the current and was whirled away.

The warriors began to draw back. They were still dangerous, since their arrows were not yet used up. Perley Wright got one of the shafts in the shoulder, and was out of the fight. Screams of pain testified to horses hit. But the wagon was now on firm bottom. With terror Esty saw that Captain Mabbitt had the reins. Where was

Beaver Jim Jones? Then the boy saw him with a feathered arrow sticking out from his body. Esty shut his eyes and turned away.

As in a sick dream he heard his fellows passing the low-voiced news. Emory Clarke and Yankee Soule were dead. The others had tried to bring away the bodies, but had all they could do to drag in Beaver Jim and Anson Gregory, who were helpless. Captain Mabbitt's right cheek was "burned" by a bullet, and Gid Prouty was bleeding profusely from a scalp wound. Esty could think of nothing but that hideous shaft buried in his friend's chest.

No sooner had he got to shore than he toppled from Whiskers' back in a dead faint. When he came to, he was gasping from the effects of a bucket of water over his head. Beaver Jim Jones was standing near, holding the iron-stiff doeskin coat in one hand and in the other the blunted arrow which had done him no worse damage than a severe jab in the ribs. He was saying ruefully:

"Best bedotched jacket ever I owned in my life. And now the thing is plumb sp'iled."

CHAPTER 14

The Patron

THE immediate danger was over. Sixteen dead Pawnees were scattered on the flat which the atajo had just quitted. Many others must have been wounded. After so sharp a lesson, the Indians' appetite for fighting would be poor.

The old Chouteau fortification was in fair shape. Back of it, Captain Mabbitt's men could defend the island successfully. If it was to be a siege, they were well fixed. Grass for the animals was plentiful. The river was full of fish. They could hold out for a long time. It was a pleasant place to rest. But they were in that country for fur, not rest. They wanted to be "on our way to Santa Fe" as they had so often sung. The

152

Pawnees stood in the path. To attempt a re-
crossing in the face of that army would have
been suicide.

The atajo was now reduced to twelve men,
thirty-five animals and two wagons. Captain
Mabbitt's Conestoga from which Esty had made
his escape was wedged on a sandbank in midstream, half a mile below. The Indians had
made no attempt to get it off.

For two weeks the Mabbitt men loafed on the
island. It was a restless and unhappy time.
Tempers were quick. The members grumbled
against the discipline. They talked of making a
night attack. They discussed building a raft on
the far side of the island and escaping to the
north shore, abandoning their equipment. Captain Mabbitt vetoed it. There they would stay
and wait out the Indians.

On a warm and misty October night there
was much activity in the Pawnee camp. It
might mean an attack in the darkness. Instead,
when the sun rose, it revealed an astonishing
spectacle. Not an Indian remained on the flats.
They had quietly decamped. In their place was
a group of a dozen men and as many mules. A
pole had been set up in the sand. From it flew
a flag with a device: an animal in red cloth on

a background of white. Gid Prouty recognized
it.

"The beaver flag," he told his companions.
"They must be Auguste Chouteau's Frenchies."

A man came to the brink of the river and
shouted through his cupped hands. Captain
Mabbitt beckoned him to come over. The whole
band mounted and urged their horses into the
ford. As they landed on the island, Esty looked
them over. They were not large men, but they
looked lean and wiry and alert. All were heavily
bearded. The weapons which they carried were
better than those of Mabbitt's men. They dismounted, grouped together and murmured in
French among themselves. Their headman came
forward and shook hands with Captain Mabbitt.
His name, he said, was Pierre Chaffard.

"What became of the Indians?" the captain
asked.

"We told them to go. They went," the
Frenchman said.

"Without a fight?" the leader asked, puzzled.
"They were twenty to your one."

"They respect our flag," the other said. "Here
the Patron's word is law."

It struck Esty, listening with all his ears, that
Mr. Chouteau, whom this man called "the

Patron," must be a very powerful person. Now Captain Mabbitt was asking whether the Frenchmen had known about the atajo. Yes, Chaffard said, two of the Chouteau trappers, working in the vicinity, had heard shots, watched the battle, and made a five-day journey upstream, to their main fort, to report to the Patron. The Patron had sent him back with his little force to rescue the whites.

"Thanks," Captain Mabbitt said. "We needed it."

"You go to Santa Fe?" the Frenchman asked.

"Yes."

"Go quickly."

Captain Mabbitt's peculiarly set eyes snapped cross fires. "Who says so?"

"Auguste Chouteau. This is his fur country."

"This is the United States of America," the captain retorted with emphasis. "We are Americans. Nobody is going to run us out of our own country."

"It is an order," the other said quietly.

The leader looked at his little group which had gathered about him with darkening faces. They were outnumbered. The Chouteau men had better weapons and undoubtedly more powder and lead.

"I figured to have to fight Injuns," he said with a rueful shake of his head. "I didn't reckon I'd have to fight white men."

Gid Prouty spoke up. "I thought this Chouteau was an American, himself. What kind of way is this to treat other Americans?"

The Frenchman became apologetic. "Three of you Americans came up from Santa Fe," he said. "The Patron welcomed them kindly. They brought with them the spotted disease. Our men broke out in angry spots. Some died. The Patron, who fears nothing else on earth, has a terror of that sickness. He wants no more disease-bearing strangers in his country."

"Brought the smallpox up from Santa Fe, did they?" Captain Mabbitt said thoughtfully.

"With two friends I myself went to Santa Fe, seeking the magic powder which is potent against the disease."

"Kine-pox," the leader said.

"There was none left, though I offered gold for it. None!"

"Take me to see this Patron of yours."

"He will not wish to see you. He does not wish to see anyone."

"I could maybe fix him up," Captain Mabbitt said. "I've got kine-pox enough for his outfit."

The Frenchman seized him by the arm. "Then we go. We start. Toute suite. Immedia-ment!"

There were matters to be attended to first, Captain Mabbitt insisted. It was "picks and spades" again; this time for a sad task. The two dead companions were buried and a service said over them. The lost wagon was still grounded on the sand bar. All available ropes were spliced together. Looping one end about his shoulders, Esty swam out to the place from the nearest point and made fast to the wagon tongue. Two of the most reliable mules were hitched to the shore end. After some careful maneuvering, Esty got the wagon into the water. The rest was easy.

So impatient was Chaffard that Captain Mab-bitt consented to ride on ahead with him, leav-ing the slower wagons to follow. Esty, Sid Danby, and Doggo McIntyre were taken along as exhibits. Pushing on for long hours, they made the five-day journey in a little more than three.

Auguste Chouteau, spare, dignified and mid-dle-aged, received them with austere reserve. He made no attempt to conceal his suspicions. He knew something of the miracle of kine-pox, having learned of it on his latest trip to St. Louis. No; he had never been vaccinated himself. He wished now that he had been. How was he to know that this stranger's powder was the genuine kine-pox?

"Shuck those coats, boys," the captain directed his followers.

All three took off their jackets and rolled up their left sleeves. The Patron examined their arms, one after the other. Esty's and Sid's showed fine, dead-white blotches, but it was Doggo's scar that settled the Patron's doubts. It was still angry red around the edges because Doggo had not been able to refrain from scratching the place. The Patron bared his arm.

"Proceed, Doctor," he said.

With the solemnity proper to so great an occasion, the operator unsheathed his skinning knife, whetted it on a stone, super-whetted it on his own horny palm, and went at the job.

Three days later, the place was itching magnificently. The patient was delighted. All of his men should undergo the treatment. What was the charge?

"A mule," Captain Mabbitt answered blandly.

"That's where I thought we'd get run right

out of camp," Doggo confided to Esty after-
ward. "A mule apiece for putting a few scratches
on a man's arm. Though we sure did need the
mules!"

It was, indeed, an outrageous charge. The
Patron did not so much as blink. A vaccination
party was held then and there, and the Mabbitt
atajo was richer by sixteen good mules from the
camp's breeding pen. Monsieur Chouteau
would have bought the six remaining doses of
the powder, but Esty whispered to Captain Mabbitt to hold it. The smallpox had come from
Santa Fe; probably there would be a demand for
the kine-pox there.

The wagon train came in five days later. It
was greeted by the good news that the country
was open to the Mabbitt men. They could hunt
and trap where they pleased. Nothing, said
Auguste Chouteau, gently rubbing his red-hot
arm, was too good for them.

So many furs were brought in and packaged
in the next two months that the four wagons
and all the mule packs could not begin to hold
them. The atajo decided to build a company
wagon. Partisan Carr, who claimed to have been
a wheelwright back East, was put in charge of
the work. Everybody helped and gave advice.

The result was astonishing. It looked more like an oversized pianoforte box than a vehicle. For wheels it had four matched chunks of hardwood tree trunks. Its maximum speed over level ground was two miles an hour, and the sound of its progress was like a thunderstorm among hills. Mules are not sensitive animals, and the eight that were hitched to "Carr's chariot" were

specially tough. They went on strike when first they heard that awful slam-bang-whang at their heels.

With all its faults, the chariot had room for a lot of trade. It was the joint property of the atajo. Each member was to pay into the common money-box rental for the space he took up.

At first Esty intended to bid for a large space to carry his two bales of beaver and one of otter. He had a second thought which he confided to his friend, the madre.

"Gid, how much do you reckon a shelf in the chariot will rent for?"

"All it's wuth. Maybe more," the cook replied.

"Got any extra room in the cook wagon?"

"Not a square inch. Nor nobody else."

"I've been doing some thinking about this fur trade," the boy said.

"Don't strain yourself, Muley," his friend advised.

"Those men that brought the smallpox in; they were from Santa Fe."

"So that Frenchy told us."

"How do we know that other fur parties from there haven't been trapping this territory?"

"Sposen they have?"

"There'll be plenty of pelts on the market there. Ours won't fetch what they would at home."

"Nothin' wrong with your arithmetic, Muley," said the madre admiringly.

"So, I'm not going to rent any wagon space."

"What'll you do with your pelts?"

"Swap 'em. Right here. With the other men."

"For what?"

"Anything that don't take up so much room that I can't pack it on one mule." Esty had already bought Whiskers from its owner. "I'll put my price for skins so low they'll grab at it. Two dollars a pound for prime pelts. And look what I'll save on the wagon rent."

Mr. Gideon Prouty's reasoning powers were also in good working order. "You better rent yourself some space just the same, Muley," he advised.

"Why should I?"

"Because if you don't, every man in the atajo will know you got no way to get your stuff to market. They'll say, 'Take our price or let your pelts rot on the ground.' You'll get shillings where you reckoned on dollars."

"Gid," Esty said after a pause, "sometimes I think I'm not as smart as I thought I was."

"Keep right on thinkin' that way, and you won't be a tenderfoot no longer, Muley," said the madre encouragingly.

Every evening after cleaning up, Esty traded. The other members winked at one another. They thought the boy was soft in the head to let his good furs go so low. The young trader kept resolutely to his idea of small stuff. Trinkets. Notions. Ribbons. Pins by the dozen. Candle wicking. Bits of chalk. A few spools of silk thread. (He got his money back fifty times over on those.) Half a dozen small, circular hand mirrors. (They went like wildfire at Santa Fe.) All the string he could pick up. Ropes and lariats.

"Goin' to start a junk shop, Muley?" the madre asked as Esty's hoard piled up.

Six of the vaccine tubes were left. Esty tackled the captain. How much for half of them?

"If it wasn't for you, I'd have lost the whole box," the leader said. "So maybe you reckon I'd ought to give 'em to you for nothing." His eyes twinkled. "Trade's trade and this is a tradin' outfit. Ounce of gold apiece for the three."

More than forty dollars. A heavy price, but Esty paid it in skins.

There came a day when the atajo could pack no more. They set out for Santa Fe. At the last stop, the village of San Miguel, they had disturbing news. The governor of the province, Don Manuel Armijo did not like Americans. He was already informed of their approach. He was eager for trade; the whole city was; but they might find him a hard man to deal with.

Captain Mabbitt was impressed. Instead of going direct into the city, he halted his caravan at an abandoned silver mine on a hillside. Taking Esty and Beaver Jim Jones with him, he rode forward, leaving the rest of the company to guard the wagons.

CHAPTER 15

Santa Fe

Looking down upon the city from muleback, Esty was disappointed. The magnificent metropolis, as it had been described to him, was a patchwork of mean little mud huts centering upon a plaza where the cathedral stood. Not much prospect of trade there, he thought.

The principal industries of the place, as far as he could make out as he rode into the great square, were casting dice, playing cards, and sleeping in the shade. A company of soldiers armed chiefly with short bows and long lances, were languidly drilling on a littered parade ground.

A tall, gaunt man with a leathery face and

165

tired eyes rose from a bench and addressed the leader.

"You Salt Lick Mabbitt? Glad to see you. I'm Caleb Tompkins."

The captain shook hands with him. "How come you know me?" he asked.

"Couple of caballeros reported you from Cimarron Crossing last fall. What can I do for you?"

"I'd like to see the governor."

Mr. Tompkins shook his head. "Wait a little. You'll see his Minister of Finance soon enough. He's at my house, expecting you. Come along. I'll be your interpreter."

On the way he told the newcomer that there were twenty Americans and Englishmen, trappers and prospectors in the city. The governor, who was a bad-mannered, ill-tempered Mexican, did not like them. He did not like any foreigners.

Mr. Tompkins' house was an adobe structure, larger and cleaner than most. As they entered, a splendid figure rose and bowed. He carried a silver-mounted sword and wore a gorgeous uniform. The front of his coat was covered with gold braid, medals, and grease spots. He was introduced as Señor Valmonte.

The señor welcomed the stranger in a flowery speech. He understood that El Capitan Mabbitt's atajo brought rich and valuable trade in wagons. Was this true?

Yes, the captain said, they did bring trade.

Wonderful, the Finance Minister cried. Nobody had ever before come in from the north in wagons. Little trade of any kind had entered since the glorious revolution that had freed Mexico from Spain. Fine prices could be had for merchandise. There would also be a modest tax.

"How much?" Captain Mabbitt inquired when this was translated.

"Five hundred dollars gold per wagon," the official answered.

"*What?*" the captain shouted.

"And a twenty-five per cent tariff on all goods sold," the señor added cheerfully.

The visitor turned a deep red. "Tell him," he instructed his interpreter, "that I'll turn around and take the atajo back to the United States before I pay his blasted tax."

"He says," Mr. Tompkins returned after delivering the message, "that His Excellency's gallant and glorious army would not permit the removal of untaxed goods. You will have three days to consider, after which your goods will be confiscated."

"Robbery!" the captain stormed. "What can I do?" he asked Mr. Tompkins.

"You can't fight his army," the American replied. "They'd starve you out. It's a dirty mulk. But I guess they've got you."

While the three men discussed the situation to one side, Esty had politely introduced himself to the official. At San Miguel he had heard some interesting rumors. Now he wished to follow them up. Was there a licensed physician in the city, he asked Señor Valmonte. Certainly. Dr. Castro: a learned man, educated in Europe and official doctor to the governor's household. Was the young gentleman not feeling well? The young gentleman was feeling perfectly well, but he had other reasons which he did not mention for wishing to see the doctor. The señor gave him directions and Esty set out.

Dr. Castro's waiting room was crowded, but the arrival of a traveler from the United States was such an event that Esty was shown in at once. He liked the looks of the physician at first sight: a small, alert, vigorous man with kindly eyes. A man to be trusted, Esty thought. Anyhow, Esty had to trust him if his plan was to be

worked out. Dr. Castro asked the visitor what
ailed him.

"Nothing," Esty said.

"Then why have you come to me?"

For answer, Esty stripped off his jacket and
exhibited his vaccination mark. With an exclamation, the doctor did the same. They smiled
broadly at one another and shook hands. Those
scars were a sort of badge, making them, as it
might be, brothers of a fraternity.

"How much kine-pox have you, Doctor?" the
caller asked.

"None," was the reply which Esty expected
and hope for. "There is none in the province;
none in all Mexico. I have sent to England for
a supply, but who knows when it will come?
This month? Next month? Next year? Perhaps
never."

The time had come for open dealing, Esty
decided. "I've got three doses," he said. "Captain Mabbitt's got another three."

The doctor grabbed Esty by the shoulders.
"Where are they? Give them to me. How much?
Name your price. Anything!"

"You want it for the governor, don't you?"
Esty asked shrewdly. "I heard something in San
Miguel."

Dr. Castro excitedly confirmed it. His Excellency's older daughter had been stricken several weeks before. She had recovered, but was so hideously pitted that she would go nowhere in public. Now it was feared that the younger daughter might suffer the same fate.

"His Excellency knows of the learned Dr. Jenner's wonder-working discovery," the physician said. "There is nothing he would not give to have his child safeguarded. Himself, also. I implore you to let me have at least one powder at any price you name."

"I'll give you my three," Esty said.

The physician stared at him, stupefied. "You'll *give* them?"

"If you will get the governor to let our wagons in, tax free."

He explained the situation. Captain Mabbitt, Esty said, would never submit to that tax. He would turn around and go back first. And if anybody tried to stop him, he and his men would fight. Thus it had become a matter of life or death to the atajo.

Dr. Castro listened gravely. He understood, he said, and he did not blame Captain Mabbitt. He was sure that the governor would agree. He would agree to anything in order to get that

precious kine-pox. The doctor's face darkened.
He came close to his visitor and spoke in his ear.

"He will agree. But would he hold to his
agreement? After the señorita is vaccinated and
the danger over, what is to prevent Don Manuel
from seizing your goods anyway?" He added, "If
it were known that I have spoken thus of
him . . ." He drew his finger across his throat in
a meaningful gesture.

After much argument and persuasion, Dr.
Castro consented to a secret meeting with Captain Mabbitt and Beaver Jim Jones. The scheme
which they finally worked out to insure that the
governor would keep his pledge was mainly Mr.
Jones's. It was risky. But any other course was
certain disaster. Dr. Castro went to the palace to
tell the governor that Captain Mabbitt himself
would vaccinate the señorita when the governor gave his word to let the whole pack train in,
free. The others returned to the silver mine.

There the whole supply of kine-pox, except
one tube, was carried out at night and quietly
buried. The one tube was taken to Gid Prouty's
cook wagon where a change of contents was
secretly made. The men sat up late composing a
letter which Esty put into Spanish.

Word came from Dr. Castro early the next

morning. Don Manuel agreed to everything.
Would El Capitan Mabbitt return with the
messenger and perform the operation? He did
so. The wailing and terrified child was duly
vaccinated in the presence of her father. At the
finish he grunted something which might have
been thanks, and shuffled out of the room.

Hardly had the captain got back to his companions at the mine, when the Minister of
Finance appeared with an armed escort. He had
come to notify El Captain that the tax must be
paid before sunset.

"That's all fixed," Captain Mabbitt told
Señor Valmonte through Esty. "The tax is off.
The governor has given his promise."

"Some mistake," the Minister of Finance replied blandly. "The tax stands. His Excellency
has sent me here to inform you of it. And," he
added significantly "you are fortunate that your
entire property is not forfeited."

Dr. Castro had been right in his suspicions.

Excusing himself for the moment, Captain
Mabbitt went to his wagon and returned with
the letter over which the conspirators had
burned several buffalo-tallow candles the night
before. The letter, in the most formal Spanish
at Esty's command, read to this effect:

Captain Mabbitt's compliments to His Excellency, Don Manuel Armijo, and he hoped that
what followed would be acceptable. Fearing
that there might be some misunderstanding
about the terms of the agreement, El Capitan
had ventured a slight change in the arrange-
ments. Don Manuel's little daughter had been
vaccinated not with kine-pox but with a harm-
less mixture of white flour and bleached
mustard.

El Capitan would be delighted to perform a
genuine vaccination with guaranteed kine-pox

on the following terms. His Excellency would sign the enclosed agreement, with official seal. He would then go to the cathedral and take public oath to carry out its terms on peril of his immortal soul. With Captain Mabbitt's respectful assurances of his personal regard and esteem, he remained etc. etc.

"And I hope he chokes when he reads it," the captain had added as he signed his name to the letter.

The governor very nearly did choke. Gossip of the town said that, on reading it, he turned purple, foamed at the mouth, and ended by drawing his sword and chasing the terrified Finance Minister halfway across the plaza.

He went to the cathedral, however, and took an oath that he would not have dared to violate.

His little girl was revaccinated and she shrieked louder than before. Dr. Castro had his much-desired three tubes of vaccine. In the interests of good feeling, Captain Mabbitt agreed to pay a tax of ten per centum on all sales made by the atajo. As it turned out, the men could well afford it.

All Santa Fe, it seemed to Esty, was waiting in the plaza when the wagons rolled in, followed by the pack mules. The resident Americans

were there and helped to form a guard. It was
necessary. There had been a trade famine in the
place for months. The townspeople were like a
pack of hungry wolves.

At first sight of the city Esty had been struck
by its apparent poverty. Now he was impressed
by its wealth. Everybody had money. Or, if not
money, something else just as good: opals, turquoises, peridots, jade, and gold dust. Pande-
monium broke out as soon as the wagonmen
laid out their goods. It was the most disorderly
market that Esty had ever seen.

A citizen would lay hold on a five-yard swatch
of cotton. "How much?"

The owner, instructed by Caleb Tompkins
in local business methods, would answer,
"What'll you give?"

"Three pesos a yard." The bidder then held
up three fingers as indication. This would have
been a fine profit. Before the seller could accept
it, another Mexican shoved the first aside and
seized the cloth.

"Five pesos," he shouted.

A fat woman in rags waved a purse crammed
with money. "I give seven in coined silver."

"Do not listen to her. She is a sorceress. I offer
ten."

"Eleven here." "Twelve." "Fifteen." It was like an auction gone mad. The goods were pulled this way and that. The local Americans were driven crazy, trying to interpret for everybody. In the melee a keg of nails was tipped over, spilling its contents on the ground. There was a screaming rush for the place. People grabbed up the bits of metal by the handful, forcing coins on the nearest American. They paid five, six, seven cents apiece for the nails.

Silks went for twenty-five dollars a yard. Tobacco brought three dollars a pound. A gay but-

ton with a star or a flower design in the glass could be traded even for a good opal. Mirrors, soap, pepper, paper, tar, candles, knives, tools of any kind, were grabbed at prices which made the sellers' eyes bulge. Captain Mabbitt had figured on doubling his money. Many of the goods brought in ten, fifteen, even twenty times their original cost. Esty's knickknacks were making him rich by the minute.

Sam Mullins had brought in a stock of ladies' hats trimmed with silk. That started the riot. At first sight there was a feminine rush. Fights

broke out. The bargain hunters clawed and spit and kicked and bit. A squad of soldiers was called to restore order. The soldiers dropped their weapons and joined the scrabble. They had wives at home, and nothing so fashionable as that headgear had been seen in Santa Fe for many a long year.

Looting became general. Out of the corner of his eye Esty saw a wrinkled old crone snatch a broom from the tail flap of Mr. Jones's wagon. He made a dive for her. She clasped the broom to her bosom and set off across the square, screeching like a witch. Just as the pursuer reached for her, a Mexican who had been taking his siesta with his back against a tree, thrust out his leg. Esty took a high dive and rolled. When he got the dust out of his eyes, he saw the fugitive duck through a door.

Angry and determined now, he ran to the place and began to kick at the door. After a moment it was opened. The old woman stood there, smiling a toothless smile and holding out a robin's egg turquoise, rough set in silver. The broom stood in the corner.

"Para swap?" she inquired in a wheedling voice.

The gem looked to be worth twelve or fifteen

dollars. The broom had cost maybe six bits at Barney's store. Esty took the turquoise, said, "Gracias, señora," and left.

The tumult was over when he returned to the plaza. No merchandise remained on the ground. What the Americans could rescue from the grasping hands was stowed in the wagons. Nearly a quarter of the stuff, besides what was paid for, had been carried off, Mr. Jones told him sourly. A complaint had been made to the governor; not that it would do any good. These Mexicanos were a lot of thieves. Mr. Jones was for packing everything and going back to the abandoned mine.

Caleb Tompkins advised against it. Mr. Jones and his fellows did not understand the Mexicans. "Wait and see," said Mr. Tompkins.

The first looter to return was a young and skittish señorita. She was wearing two hats, for which she wished to pay. There was no intention of theft in her mind, she explained; she had taken the hats to keep them away from that envious cat, her neighbor, Señora Fuera. The señorita was followed by a man with a spade, a youth with a pocketful of nails, a soldier who wished to settle for two cans of pepper and a mop, and a minor official with a candle mold.

The next day they opened market again, sold the rest of their merchandise and all their furs. Beaver and otter did not bring top prices, but there was still a profit. Three times Esty checked and rechecked his figures before he could believe his addition. Even then he asked the obliging Mr. Tompkins to verify it. The atajo had taken in twenty-two thousand dollars in cash and an estimated seven thousand in valuables. Esty, when his debts were paid, would be worth nearly three thousand dollars. He could buy a wagon—two wagons—five wagons. He could buy horses and mules. He could carry his own trade. Esty Lang, trader!

The atajo spent a pleasant and restful two weeks in Santa Fe. Partisan Carr, Sam Mullins and Doggo McIntyre decided to settle and operate from there. Gee-haw Johnson and Sid Danby liked what they had heard of gold strikes along the Picketwire. They would try their luck up country. But not in wagons. Pack train was good enough for them.

The rest held council with Mr. Tompkins and some of the prospectors. They had brought their wagons through triumphantly, but none of them had any wish to repeat the bitter hardships of the river gorge with its blockading rocks. Mr. Tompkins strongly advised the Cimarron route, down the Cimarron River to the last water; then strike due north. With a compass they could not miss the Arkansas River.

"Across the Jornada del Muerto?" said Captain Mabbitt. "We lost a wagon outfit and three men there coming down. And," he glanced at Esty, "nearly another member."

"The wagon was found last month," Mr. Tompkins said gravely. "The skeletons, men and animals, were a few miles away."

"They were looking for Cibola," Esty said, "the Lost Cities."

"There is no Cibola," the other said. "It's a myth, a legend, a dangerous lie. Too many men, believing it, have lost their lives."

Through the dust-filled sunshine of Franklin a battered Pittsburgh wagon rumbled on a May morning of 1823. It carried a fine assortment of beaver pelts picked up on the eastward journey, and its two owners. On the canvas side was painted large and clear:

JONES & LANG
Furs and Trade
Big Muddy to Santa Fe

It stopped at the post office. The younger member of the firm delivered to Postmistress Huff a carefully drawn map to be tacked up on the wall for the free use of westbound atajos. Across that part of it marked "Jornada del Muerto," the route was heavily inked in with crossbars every two miles, indicating landmarks set up by the travelers.

"Follow the Marks," the legend read. "They Will Lead You From Water to Water."

That was the beginning of the Santa Fe Trail.